What the critics

'Funny and unsettling
a fine addition to Dre
Matthew Co

'Expansive, perfectly controlled, almost achingly painful,
it shows Drewe at the height of his powers.'
James Bradley, AUSTRALIAN LITERARY REVIEW

'*The Rip* is incredibly good – dazzling. These stories lie
in wait for the reader. They're wonderful.'
Brenda Walker

'There are few writers who can match Drewe's delicate balance of
comedy and tragedy… the bedrock of the power of his writing.'
ADELAIDE ADVERTISER

'One of Australia's finest writers returns to familiar territory with
even greater skill, wit, pathos and marvellous economy of language.'
Lucy Clark, SUNDAY TELEGRAPH

'A delight… He has a laid-back clarity of vision that makes you
want to look at the world again to see what you missed.'
Christopher Bantick, SUNDAY TASMANIAN

'A fully rewarding collection of stories… the best we've got.'
Malcolm Knox, SYDNEY MORNING HERALD

'Drewe drills down into the emotions of middle Australians.
He entices readers with simplicity, then belts them with significance.'
WEEKEND AUSTRALIAN

ALSO BY ROBERT DREWE

The Savage Crows
A Cry in the Jungle Bar
The Bodysurfers
Fortune
The Bay of Contented Men
Our Sunshine
The Drowner
Walking Ella
The Shark Net
Grace
Montebello
The Local Wildlife

PLAYS
The Bodysurfers – The Play
South American Barbecue

AS EDITOR
The Penguin Book of the Beach
The Penguin Book of the City
Best Australian Stories 2006
Best Australian Stories 2007
Best Australian Essays 2010

ROBERT DREWE

The Rip

*To Matt & Lucy
Xmas 2017
Love
Roger.*

PENGUIN BOOKS

PENGUIN BOOKS

Published by the Penguin Group
Penguin Group (Australia)
707 Collins Street, Melbourne, Victoria 3008, Australia
(a division of Penguin Australia Pty Ltd)
Penguin Group (USA) Inc.
375 Hudson Street, New York, New York 10014, USA
Penguin Group (Canada)
90 Eglinton Avenue East, Suite 700, Toronto, Canada ON M4P 2Y3
(a division of Penguin Canada Books Inc.)
Penguin Books Ltd
80 Strand, London WC2R 0RL England
Penguin Ireland
25 St Stephen's Green, Dublin 2, Ireland
(a division of Penguin Books Ltd)
Penguin Books India Pvt Ltd
11 Community Centre, Panchsheel Park, New Delhi – 110 017, India
Penguin Group (NZ)
67 Apollo Drive, Rosedale, Auckland 0632, New Zealand
(a division of Penguin New Zealand Pty Ltd)
Penguin Books (South Africa) (Pty) Ltd
Rosebank Office Park, Block D, 181 Jan Smuts Avenue, Parktown North,
Johannesburg 2196, South Africa
Penguin (Beijing) Ltd
7F, Tower B, Jiaming Center, 27 East Third Ring Road North, Chaoyang District,
Beijing 100020, China

Penguin Books Ltd, Registered Offices: 80 Strand, London, WC2R 0RL, England

First published by Penguin Group (Australia), 2008
This edition published by Penguin Group (Australia), 2009

7 9 10 8

Copyright © Robert Drewe 2008

The moral right of the author has been asserted

All rights reserved. Without limiting the rights under copyright reserved above,
no part of this publication may be reproduced, stored in or introduced into a retrieval
system, or transmitted, in any form or by any means (electronic, mechanical,
photocopying, recording or otherwise), without the prior written permission
of both the copyright owner and the above publisher of this book.

Design by John Canty © Penguin Group (Australia)
Cover photograph 'Red Bathers', 2001, from the series *Watercolours* by Narelle Autio
Represented by Stills Gallery, Sydney
Typeset in 11.5/18 Adobe Garamond by Post Pre-press Group, Brisbane, Queensland
Printed and bound in Australia by McPherson's Printing Group,
Maryborough, Victoria

National Library of Australia
Cataloguing-in-Publication data:

Drewe, Robert
The rip / Robert Drewe.
9780143009665 (pbk.)
Short stories, Australian – 21st century – Collections.

A823.3

penguin.com.au

For
Julie Gibbs,
Michael Bisits
and
Andrew Clark

So we beat on, boats against the current,
borne back ceaselessly into the past

F. SCOTT FITZGERALD
The Great Gatsby

Contents

The Lap Pool *1*
The Obituary of Gina Lavelle *37*
Sea Level *47*
The Water Person and the Tree Person *55*
The Whale Watchers *69*
Stones Like Hearts *77*
The Aquarium at Night *85*
Masculine Shoes *115*
The Cartoonist *135*
Prometheus and Greg *145*
How to Kill a Cane Toad *163*
The Rip *183*
The Life Alignment of the Coffee Grower *193*

The Lap Pool

NAKED AND FORTY-SEVEN, Leon K. backstroked steadily up and down his lap pool, an eddy of drowned insects in his wake. Of course he knew his rhythm by now; he automatically counted strokes as well as laps. Each of the forty laps that added up to one kilometre took him fifteen strokes. On each fifteenth backward reach he trusted that the fingertips of his right hand rather than the back of his skull would strike the wall first. Stroking, breathing, stroking, breathing, he swam almost in a trance.

Despite the pool's cool temperature (it was a windy autumn and the connection to the solar panels on the farmhouse roof was broken) he needed to swim in order to relax, to cope, to live the current version of his life. He swam as early dawn rays struck the surface and again as the shadows of the palms crisscrossed the pool in the late afternoon. Nowadays he preferred backstroke, and swimming naked made him feel momentarily free of his current restraints. (It wasn't as if anyone was likely to drop by.) Swimming on his back was also therapeutic; there were the clouds to observe through the palm fronds, and swifts scooting and flicking after insects, and kestrels hovering like hang-gliders over the orchard. In its constancy this silent aerial activity was immensely soothing. There was always at least one bird somewhere in the sky.

A Google search attested to the State swimming successes of his youth. Thirty years later he was a tall, keg-chested man with arms and legs less disproportionately long than they'd seemed back then. A more bowed and slope-shouldered specimen, too, he'd noticed lately, more weighed down by the gravity of anxious time and snowballing events than even a year ago.

His sixth month alone and the farm was so quiet these afternoons just before the cockatoo clamour of sunset that from the pool Leon K. could hear his daughters' downcast ponies tearing grumpily at the grass in the home paddock. Awaiting his trial, which had been adjourned for yet another four months while the authorities strengthened their case against him, he swam his two lap sessions and paced his overgrown boundaries, scrutinising nature. The rest of the time, or during the region's frequent electrical storms, he restlessly roamed his veranda, by day with a pot of green tea and a sudoku puzzle, by night with a bottle of his cellar's dwindling supply of merlot or pinot noir.

By now all the official delays, court adjournments and tax investigations were jumbled together in his mind. The future appeared increasingly hazy and he felt the same fatalistic confusion he knew on that dip in the coast highway near Sugar Cane Road, when night sea-fogs suddenly swept over the cane fields. What should he anticipate around the next murky bend? A riskily unlit hippie cyclist, an invisible hitchhiker, a petrol tanker thundering across the imperceptible lane markings? Would he ever see his way clear?

Against his own best interests he'd come to dread the weekly visit of the one person who might at least clarify matters for him, his solicitor, Gareth Wyntuhl. As the legal process dragged on, he increasingly resented spending every Thursday afternoon and Friday on the lawyer's highly expensive devil's advocacy and narrow legalistic interpretation of the prosecution case. He also resented him for eating into his swimming time. This wasn't strictly true. He still swam his usual laps, though less calmly with Wyntuhl hovering enigmatically at the pool edge, whistling tunelessly through his teeth and forever looking at his watch. With the lawyer present, he felt bound to don his Speedos – and resented not swimming naked, too.

Unavoidably these days, after an hour or so in the lawyer's presence he lapsed into a mild fugue. On a bad day Wyntuhl's monotone could make his brain shut down completely. At the start of his troubles he'd tried to fight the unusual effect it had on him: the gradual fainting sensation and cloudy vision, leading to a total mental fade-out, a sort of grey noise where only background sounds had any relevance. The tap-tapping of the pool's filter box, magpies calling on the lawn, brush turkeys scratching in the shrubbery. Now he went with it. It wasn't unpleasant, it was almost a reverie, and he wondered whether it felt like this to be hypnotised. Maybe Wyntuhl should grow a goatee and get himself a stage act. When he fell deeper into this particular stupor – a sort of painless, aura-free migraine – everything about Wyntuhl, from his endomorphic physical outline to the veranda table he'd heaped with files (the lawyer's attempt to claim his attention with a crisp conference ambience), faded into the rural hum and buzz and became as abstract and misty as dreams.

After the past year of examinations and committal proceedings it wasn't surprising his mind needed a rest. Tired of raking through the ashes of disgrace, his brain had called a halt. Maybe he was having a mental breakdown. How easy it was to forget the minutiae of the case – the dates, the amounts, the stock transfers and telescoping bank loans, all that paper-shuffling – and sink back into the vibrations of trees, livestock and wildlife, of cattle lowing, water dragons scuttling under the veranda, and palms rattling in the wind. Pulling this blanket of nature around his shoulders, he felt safely hidden, a snug wombat in its hole. Somehow less ignoble, he could even fantasise about the puzzling uniqueness of his position. Instead of a former company director under indictment for alleged 'corporate misconduct' and 'breaches of directors' duties', he could be a beleaguered sovereign awaiting news from the front. Maybe a Caribbean president anticipating a peasant uprising from the sugarcane fields below.

If only the calm didn't end at the last lap, at the moment his fingertips tipped the wall behind him and he stood, removed his goggles and allowed the dusk's pink-grey shadows to settle on his body for a few seconds. But, inevitably, reality returned. He stepped heavily out of the pool, shivering now and streaming water, and stamped bare-arsed across the terrace to the house.

※

Lushly green, thanks to their prime position between the coast and the Nightcap Ranges, his thirty-two acres lay along a north–south valley of carved-up dairy farms, formerly dense rainforest known as the Big Scrub. Cleared of its native red cedars a century ago, the rich volcanic soil now nurtured in their place a thriving feral tree, the camphor laurel, imported from China during a nineteenth-century preoccupation with arboreal neatness. Long escaped from its municipal parks and government schoolyards, the camphor laurel now ran as wild and free as the thistle and dandelion throughout the Northern Rivers. And, disgracefully, at scenically unrestrained intervals, over Leon K.'s acres.

Of course his neighbours, real farmers, many of whose ancestors had razed the original rainforest to plant grass for their cattle, detested the camphor laurel as an alien weed, a timber version of the Asian Hordes. If he might harbour some guilt deep in his heart for his alleged misdemeanours (*uncharacteristic errors of judgement through overwork, a misplaced trust in subordinates, unforeseen vagaries in the market* were the forms of words Wyntuhl suggested to explain them) he hadn't a leaf, a twig, of environmental guilt. How could those farmers understand the quiet pleasure those camphor laurels gave him, their gentle tiers sloping and rolling away towards the cane fields and the sea? He found the trees' leafy density and undulating outlines attractively foreign. At dusk their voluptuous silhouettes filled him with nostalgia for something ordered yet indefinable: contentment, even romance.

There was a cosy childish component, too, in the trees' rounded, European appearance. His daughters used to call them 'broccoli trees', the camphor laurels reminding them of that unwelcome clumpy vegetable on their dinner plates. For him they recalled the trees in the picture books of his youth; *The Magic Faraway Tree* was a favourite. Even the word 'camphor' brought back aromatic childhood memories: his grandmother's wardrobes and linen chest in Budapest. His own camphor laurels, meanwhile, were forever striking new shoots, which he made no attempt to cut out. It was another count against him, this city gent's whimsy, a hobby-farmer's un-Australian and neglectful misuse of the land.

His property was L-shaped, with the farmhouse and his sixteen highest acres forming the vertical part of the L. On the horizontal bottom sixteen, beyond the red-clay dam and the orchard, with its rotting and desiccated fruit, his twenty-three beef cattle – a token herd to fatten and sell – grazed behind a multicoloured foreign tangle of blackberry, lantana and bougainvillea, the subject of monthly noxious-weed-action warnings from the local council. Lately, a couple of headstrong yearlings had begun squeezing through the electric fence and barbed wire into the neighbouring property. Their dopey discontent – they were happy to be zapped and lacerated every day just to sample the identical grass on the other side – astounded him at first, but no longer. That was the country for you.

He had never claimed to be any sort of farmer himself. In the first enthusiastic flush of ownership he'd keenly planted a wide sample of regional produce: mangoes, guavas, macadamia and pecan nuts, a few coffee bushes for novelty's sake, some custard apples, imaginative hybrid citrus like lemonade trees and tangelos, also papayas, bananas, lychees and avocados. He'd imagined satisfying strolls through his orchard after Sunday lunch parties, and healthy family breakfasts of his own exotic fruits: icy glasses of guava and citrus juice; mangoes sliced into clever cubes. But once the troubles began, the Sunday parties quickly fell away, and breakfast somehow never progressed beyond toast and coffee. Soon he was eating, and living, alone, and those few trees still bearing fruit were taken over by fungus and fruit fly, birds and flying foxes.

Since the sale of the yacht and the ski lodge, the farm was

his only nominal asset. The house, a century-old hardwood Queenslander, badly needed renovating, but under such close financial scrutiny he couldn't carry out the necessary repairs. The authorities were monitoring his accounts. He imagined teams of investigative accountants trawling over his petrol and grocery bills, frowning at the cheques for swimming-pool chlorine and pony feed. But frankly it wasn't just the financial block preventing him from acting on anything. It was a deep lack of will. Even a phone call to a local tradesman was a daunting prospect, requiring more mental effort than he could muster. Meanwhile, unless a southerly was blowing, the septic tank reeked intrusively, the house's timbers were peeling and cracking, and the electrical wiring was questionable; increasingly, light bulbs popped after a few days. The tennis-court lights were failing, too; the last bulb was flickering and ready to blow. But to change them would also be expensive; he'd have to call an electrician and hire a cherry picker. It hardly seemed worth the effort now that he had no tennis companions, night or day.

More importantly for his daily wellbeing, the pool – built ninety years after the house, the first, vital change he'd made

THE LAP POOL

when he'd bought the property ten years before – already required extensive doctoring. Electrical fade-outs affected its pump, the tiles were loosening and blue-green algae always threatened. He swore he could see algae spores borne on the breeze and grey fungal scales clinging to the trunks of the poolside palms, awaiting their chance to poison his water. This was one problem he knew he must act on. If the structure of his life was crumbling, the pool was the only thing keeping him sane.

~~~

His old city friends shunned him as if he were contagious. And except to complain in terse phone calls about his trespassing cattle and noxious weeds, his farmer neighbours didn't communicate with him, although most days their vehicles passed him at high speed. The shared lane to his farm was a winding tunnel of blind turns, ferny overgrowth and furry road-kill through, and over, which every other driver drove murderously fast. Whenever he went to town, purposely observing the speed limit, his car was tailgated by furious motorists, and sometimes also by mysterious white vehicles. Several times he'd noticed a white car parked in his lane while someone photographed the house and property from the front gate. When he stepped outside to question the photographer, the man (he couldn't tell if it was the same man) nonchalantly sauntered to his car and accelerated away. Some authority keeping tabs on him, he supposed. One of the many gung-ho State and Federal acronyms fighting corporate crime nowadays, all competing to capture the big-business scalps. Perhaps the prosecution or the tax office, working in cahoots. Maybe a private investigator acting for a major creditor. He'd felt paranoid the first time he spotted this overt surveillance and for several nights was unable to sleep. More fatalistic these days, he expected nothing less – and still slept badly.

As for the road-ragers, it had jolted him for a moment to think they might be financially wounded shareholders, retirees who'd lost their life savings, small mum-and-dad investors like his own *Anya* and *Apa*. Lifelong hard workers and money-savers. *Little people*, some media hacks had suggested. That thought didn't bear considering for long. No, he assured himself. They wouldn't be chasing him. He had a silent telephone number; he wasn't on the local electoral roll. Probably just impatient tradesmen – testy plumbers or electricians in a hurry to the next job or the pub. Whoever they were, most of these journeys ended with their angry horn blasts and aggressive two-finger salutes.

Nevertheless – and this was a hard-to-break habit from his swimming training of thirty years ago, an urge to become a regular Australian, a suntanned sporting champion – he hadn't given up trying to adapt to his surroundings. Early on he'd grown a beard and shelved his conservative city casual-wear of polo shirts and deck shoes for work boots, jeans and heavy hemp shirts bought from a hinterland shop called Don't Tell Mama. (The labels warned: *Do Not Consume*.) However, the change of image – the green and khaki hemp, the boots, the greying whiskers – hadn't prevented a raddled old hippie from accosting him in public.

This was in the main street during his Saturday morning shopping. Out of a weedy nook between shopfronts leapt this shoeless scarecrow, ragged and bony as *Treasure Island*'s Ben Gunn. As if some dervish-releasing button had been activated, he began whirling about on the pavement, dusty dreadlocks spinning, flailing veiny arms and kicking the air. At first Leon K. thought he was having a fit. But when the assailant swung a wild punch at him, shouting, 'Fuckin' yuppie wog! Go back home, wanker!' he had to duck. He reeled back in surprise. 'Take it easy, mate.'

People peered out from doorways and cafes. 'C'mon, I'll do ya!' The aggressor launched another childish haymaker that swiped his shoulder. Who was this lunatic? Leon K. was twice his size, with enough pent-up tension of his own to knock him back into his cave or swamp. What he did was hold him off, his pulse pounding in his ears, while he wondered what to do next. Punch him to the ground? (Self-defence, plenty of witnesses.) In another second he imagined what a delicious time the Sydney scandal sheets would have of that. (At least half of the witnesses would have camera-phones.)

Leon K. brushed him aside again as the man's nonsensical obscenities mugged the gentle weekend air (*Shithead-poofter-wog! City-dickhead!*). 'Steady, tiger. I'm a local,' he protested, mildly enough in the circumstances. Inviting the onlookers' sympathy, he forced out an indulgent laugh.

Suddenly he craved sympathy, just as he ached to broadcast the fact that this nutcase, the whole community, everyone, had got him wrong. 'My mother sewed piecework in Surry Hills,' he wanted to yell. And his father, gallant and exhausted *Apam*, a civil engineer back in Hungary, a respected *kulturmernok*, had worked two jobs round the clock in Australia – tyre re-treader in Granville, nightwatchman in Parramatta – driving his son to his daily five a.m. swimming training between shifts. 'He never had time to swim himself. Never even had time to learn how,' he could tell them. This is what he wanted to share with the onlookers: his family's noble struggle and how he was absolutely his parents' son.

But disapproval flooded the street, and it wasn't aimed at the punchy scarecrow. 'Now Sonny,' a middle-aged woman murmured. 'Don't get yourself het up, darl.' So this reeking Sonny was that protected species, a local character. Fizzing with adrenaline, Leon K. dodged his windmilling fists and pushed past him. Sonny was still dancing on his cracked and crusty feet like a manic flyweight. His clothes and bouncing dreadlocks gave off aggressive, pungent odours of smoke and sweat. 'Big-city wanker! I'll be dealing with you!'

Rather than the altercation itself, it was the unfairness of the presumption behind it that shocked him that Saturday morning. How could this feral junkie whose stink now impregnated his own clothes think he represented the city and all it stood for? He was an interloper there as well. The city – the City! – that wished not merely to punish him but to knock him out of existence.

For better or worse, he'd chosen the country. Moreover, he'd tried to experience its essence. The annual district rodeo at the showground had seemed the place to start. But if he'd expected to see Outback Australia on show he'd mistaken the event. It was more American Western. Hollywood Western. Country-and-Western Western. Everyone – men, women and tiny children – in Wrangler jeans and pearl-buttoned shirts, in boots and cowboy hats, those country-singer Stetsons that looked three sizes too big. All of them dressed to the nines in order to see cows and horses discomfiting people in a flamboyantly painful way.

While the animals took their revenge, he'd shared a bench with some rum-and-Coke-drinking rodeo wives and their squabbling children. The crowd *ooh*ed as a steer threw a rider heavily against the barrier and then trampled him. Attempting to distract the steer from the prone cowboy, the rodeo clown also caught a horn in the bum, which lifted him two metres in the air. Watching him thud to earth like a polka-dotted sack of potatoes, the smallest rodeo offspring, a boy of about five, announced grimly, 'I'm never going to ride those cows.'

Embarrassed in this company, his mother shrieked, 'Don't be a girl, Chad! I'm gonna put a dress on ya!' Her friends sniggered. Chad's mother went on, 'I'm gonna put a bra and panties on ya!' Raucous laughter from the other rodeo mothers. She was on a roll now: 'You'll be sitting down to wee next!'

This was obviously another side to the country. He seemed doomed to be confused here. Best to keep his head down. He stayed away from potential hot spots like bars and clubs to prevent any more Sonny-type blow-ups. For serenity's sake he even gave up the city newspapers and read only the local rag. Better its bluff mixture of shire jottings, vandalism round-ups, New Age guff and Beef Queen updates than feline financial gossip and always seeing his name maligned.

The countryside might have become his choice, but he hadn't chosen to live there *alone*. While he'd submerged himself in the country and his wife and daughters had remained in the city, he still clung to the belief that he and Kate weren't *separated* in the pre-divorce sense of the word. It was just that she chose not to live here – and this was where her husband had to be. She'd cited the difficulty of their daughters' schooling, plus (he could still see her pacing up and down the kitchen as she delivered this particular body blow) she needed time to 'adjust' to the scandal, and so on. And so on, and so on, all the way back down the tortuous bends of the Pacific Highway in the BMW with Jessica and Madeleine to Sydney. So his family remained in the Vaucluse house transferred to Kate's name. Her acceptably-Anglo-and-incognito maiden name, to which she'd reverted with far more readiness than he'd anticipated. Yet another knife in the gut.

Now he rarely went down to Sydney. In any case, his movements were circumscribed by his bail conditions. His only regular travel these days (he'd had to surrender his passport) was the 100-kilometre round trip twice a week to report to the nearest police station. Standing at the station counter certainly killed some more time; never less than an hour, sometimes two. All he needed to do was sign the bail-appearance form and walk out. Five minutes maximum. But in six months that had never happened, the cops being such specialists at ignoring him, acting busy and strolling about purposefully with their takeaway coffees and Big Macs. Or insisting that the relevant officer was off-duty, or that the bail-appearance forms had gone astray. Even the spottiest, most self-conscious probationary constable stared right through him. Why not? He was that most invisible of felons, the white-collar criminal. The class-loathing was palpable. Give them a local wife-basher or gang-banger any day.

In the meantime his only contact with the city and the trial was Gareth Wyntuhl. But 'Wyntuhl of My Discontent', as he thought of him, was definitely contact enough, bowling up in his hire car every Thursday morning after slumming it on Regional Express's one-class 8.10 a.m. flight from Sydney. 'A plane with propellers!' Wyntuhl never failed to exclaim, amazed at his own crazy courage.

Did Leon K. welcome the company? Not at all. Having

another man in the house was unbearable. Even such a relatively hygienic urban-middle-class specimen as Wyntuhl was an intrusion. Six months' solitude must have oversensitised him, Leon K. thought. Before Wyntuhl's visits he'd never noticed male breath or male hormonal whiffs, nor middle-aged male nostrils and ears, over-loud male laughter – and, whenever Wyntuhl did laugh, that superior nasal snort and white-coffee tongue.

Male habits made a disgusting list. The deep indentations their buttocks left in the sofa, the everlasting stink in the bathroom, the eggy detritus of their breakfast plates. Representing his gender, irritating and unaware Wyntuhl had a lot to answer for. Men were so rooted to the ground, over-earthed and overbearing. Like Wyntuhl, they were forever *at large.* They took up all the space in a room, like one overstuffed armchair too many. Christ, Leon K. wondered, how did women put up with them?

Indeed, Wyntuhl's presence pointed up the painful absence of women. More than ever, Leon K. longed for a woman's ministrations and company, an affectionate female touch. A sympathetic kiss. But even loneliness was preferable

THE LAP POOL

to another male on the premises. Each Friday evening more than the last, he counted down the minutes until Wyntuhl packed up his bag and briefcase, until his airport-bound Avis car accelerated down the driveway and was absorbed by the tunnel of verdant foliage and the gagging cries of crows.

The lawyer's last visit had brought from the city not only his cold germs (Wyntuhl couldn't stop sneezing and coughing) but news of recently increased penalties for corporate misconduct. 'In your case, we're talking maximum five years inside and a $250 000 fine,' Wyntuhl had informed him. 'Not counting the tax problems. But let's not go there right now.' He emptied his lungs into a Kleenex. 'Listen, how are those pet cows of yours? I was listening to the *Country Hour* on the car radio. Beef prices are going through the roof. Red meat's back in a big way. By the way, I've been meaning to say, do yourself a favour. Lose the beard.'

'Five years! Only criminals get five years!' Sometimes, nowadays, Leon K. didn't realise he'd spoken aloud.

'Yeah, well. Five at the most. My guess is probably less.'

≋

Finding it hard to fall asleep, then unwilling to wake, Leon K. cursed his bladder for forcing the issue, rousing him most mornings before dawn. This was the time of day – the aftermath of lustful, anxious dreams – when he most missed a woman. He missed Kate. More precisely, Kate as she used to be, the Kate of their shared youthful struggles, dreamy summers, poverty, fun and ambition. It was hard now to recall that sensual and reckless Kate. These grey pre-mornings better suited the current cold and impassive Kate, the socially humiliated Kate. The Kate who'd sobbed just before she left, 'They'll all think I'm corrupt as well.' How readily she'd fit into this landscape, where ocean and sky were often indistinguishable these autumn days and the dawn mist turned every hollow between the farm and the sea into a lake of ash. There was no horizon and the grey air was tense and heavy with frustration. But in any case she wasn't here.

Already slick with dew, the tennis court was also sheeted with snowy egret droppings. This particular dawn he was sitting on the veranda steps watching the egrets' court performance. The birds paced the surface for frogs and bugs, every so often interrupting their hunt to mate noisily and aggressively. In this bucking-and-dodging dance of food and sex, one male bird was more raucous and demanding than the others. And when the first rays speared across the court it was the rowdy fornicator who led the flock in obedient V-formation into the rising mist.

In the pale early sunshine, Leon K. trudged down to the ponies' paddock to change their rugs and throw them some hay. Out of sentimental love for his daughters he bought the horses a bale of lucerne hay every week. Increasingly forlorn nevertheless, the shaggy old Shetland had taken to obsessively scratching its hindquarters against a particular fence post. The pony's hairy rump reminded him of a fur coat, a particular woman's garment from long ago, from the days of camphor-lined wardrobes, but whose fur, or where he saw it, he couldn't recall. His mother's? Grandmother's? He remembered a real fox head peering out of a shoulder – sparkling-eyed and eerily genuine. These days he had his own resident fox. Some dawns he spotted it crossing the lawn into the lantana-bougainvillea-blackberry thicket, like a guilty teenager sneaking home late, head down, ginger pelt dishevelled from the night's anarchy.

An air of suspense always hung over his next task: to clean

the pool of its overnight denizens. What would it be this morning? The surface usually whirled with floundering creatures that had fallen in overnight, each one paddling in its own panicky circle. With the pool net he might scoop up spiders, moths, frogs, beetles, worms, cane toads; once or twice a bush rat or a half-drowned possum. Next, even more suspenseful, the check of the filter box for unwelcome occupiers. Then, the pool cleared of its bigger interlopers (only the inevitable gnats remaining), and as the sun headed higher over the first line of camphor laurels, Leon K. would step out of his clothes and mud-reddened boots and, naked and shivering, jump into the water.

However, on this late-autumn morning he was feeling off-colour (bloody Wyntuhl's cold?) and the southerly breeze seemed to pierce his lungs. Scooping up the obvious floating creatures, and weighing up whether it was sensible to swim (he hated missing that first morning kilometre), he glimpsed a ripple of activity at the deep end. Squirming from the shadow of the wall was a darker ripple, a ripple that suddenly took the form of a torn strip of tyre on the highway verge. But only for a moment. The sliver of black rubber straightened, moved assertively forward, raised its head and surged towards the shallow end. Impressively and weightlessly at ease in this pH-controlled, salt-and-chlorine swimming pool was a black snake.

The snake was so commanding of its environment it was like a mockery of itself: a wildlife-park souvenir, a plastic toy. Recognising it as a red-bellied black, however, Leon K. jumped back from the edge. Although they were common here, it still gave him a shock. Any snake, even a harmless tree snake or diamond python, had this mythical power. In summer he'd spot a snake almost every week. Whether they were dangerous or not he always gave them a wide berth and they slid harmlessly back into the shrubbery.

Indeed, he'd long anticipated finding a snake in the pool one morning: hence the extended handle on the pool net. But his chest still tightened with nerves. He suddenly ached to cough but subdued the impulse in case he agitated the snake. Circling the pool, it looked so natural, so perfectly at home. It *was* at home. According to all the wildlife books, the red-bellied black preferred to live beside water, where it could catch frogs and water rats.

No doubt about it, it had to be removed – and Leon K. decided to act. The snake was about a metre and a half long; it wasn't difficult to swing the net under it and scoop it up, tail first. It tumbled into the net surprisingly easily, a concentrated black clump. Just as easily, it immediately unravelled, paused for a second – its eyes seeking and, disconcertingly, finding the eyes of the net wielder – and sped along the pole towards him. Leon K. quickly dropped both net and snake into the pool.

Unable to concentrate on anything else, he checked regularly on the snake throughout the morning. Obviously it couldn't climb out; nevertheless, whenever it swam towards him he stepped well back from the edge. At lunchtime, while he ate his sandwich by the pool, he studied the snake, almost mesmerised by its urgent bow-wave and faint rippling wake, noting that immersion made its skin darker and glossier and that when it rested and floated, its uppermost skin faded to dull slate. But generally it kept swimming back and forth, ever seeking escape. By now it must have swum more laps than his own daily quota. Surely it couldn't keep going much longer and would soon weaken and drown.

THE LAP POOL

By mid-afternoon it was floating only half coiled, as static and dead-looking as a comma. It hadn't moved in two hours. Tentatively, he splashed the pool's surface with the carefully retrieved net, whereupon the snake plunged to the bottom and rose again, its belly flashing blood red, all springy coils and searching intent. It was an angry question mark. Again he stepped back from the edge, but the snake was already floating gracefully on the surface, conserving energy, an elongated S. Who was waiting out whom? It had been in the pool now for twelve or fourteen hours. If he was ever going to swim again, Leon K. realised he needed professional help. He consulted the phone book and discovered an organisation called The Wildlife Saviours.

≈

He was drinking his breakfast coffee at 7.30, on edge at missing yet another swim – the third lap session the snake had cost him – when a Wildlife Saviour arrived. For some reason he'd expected a man in khakis and boots, not a young woman wearing jeans and a green T-shirt, with a baby in a carry-cot. The sunlight emphasised the shine of a wide scar on her right cheek. Her straight hair fell behind her like dark water. 'You haven't injured the snake, have you?' She frowned at him. 'Some men can't help it. They're on a sacred mission to bash snakes to death.'

'I haven't harmed it.' Seeing him glance at the sleeping baby, the young woman said, 'We're all volunteers. We have to fit in the wildlife rescues with our normal lives.' She set down the carry-cot on the veranda. 'Everyone's sorry for the cuddly things when they're hurt or in trouble but snakes are just as much part of the big picture as koalas and wallabies.'

She introduced herself as China Mason. He was pleased his name seemed to mean nothing to her. Indicating the pool, he said, 'There's my problem.' The snake was noticeably more faded and listless this morning. It obviously hadn't eaten for a while: as well as losing sheen and energy its body seemed to have contracted. 'It's stressed and exhausted,' said China Mason, fitting a meshed metal trap to an aluminium pole. She opened and shut the trap from a latch on the handle. Bending over the pool, revealing a tattoo of a lyrebird low on her right hip, she took only about twenty seconds to scoop up the snake from the pool and snap the trap shut, and perhaps another minute to detach the trap from the pole and place it in the back of her van. 'We release them out in the bush,' she told him. 'But if you want I could let it go in your garden – its home territory, after all.'

'No, my snake-sympathy only goes so far.' His gratitude was almost boundless, however, and as he served her coffee on the veranda he found himself talking – and listening – more enthusiastically than he had to anyone for many months. In the beginning the conversation was of snakes, of course. Blacks, eastern browns, tigers, adders, pythons. She repeated her mantra about snakes deserving the same respect as furry marsupials. 'For a venomous snake, that one in the trap is relatively timid. It attacks humans only as a last resort.' His interest in the topic surprised him, as did the novel sound of his own animated voice. All this unaccustomed chatting to a woman was making his throat dry, and when the baby woke and started to yelp like some small bush animal itself, and China Mason said, 'Do you mind if I feed her?' his answer, 'Of course not,' came out as a croak.

An unanticipated bare breast was a shock. Although he

politely averted his eyes when she lifted up her T-shirt – not the least self-consciously – and applied the baby to her nipple, its effect was to make him stand up and offer more coffee. 'Thank you,' she said, smiling slightly. 'She's Ayeshia, by the way. Sounds like the continent but spelled differently.'

Keeping up the China connection, he supposed. He felt a little dazed. Returning with the coffee, still a little giddy but anxious not to show it, he asked whether her parents had named her China because of their admiration for the country and Chinese things.

'No, they named me Janelle.' When she was small, she explained, her father liked to call her China, as in rhyming slang: *China plate – mate*, because she always hung around him, his little pal and helper. 'Then when I was nine he went out for cigarettes, just like in a film, and never came back.'

Leon K.'s first instinct was to pat her arm or shoulder, at least register his sympathy by meeting her steady gaze with his own. But the overt breast handling – the sudden switching of sides, both nipples simultaneously visible for a moment, then the replacement of the first breast inside the T-shirt and the complete exposure of the second one for Ayeshia's benefit – hampered any such response. For a while there was a lot of fleshy bustling and bouncing going on, and of course no touch was possible. The breasts dominated the veranda, the way they introduced intimacy, presumed it, and at the same time forbade it. Anyway, she was a stranger. For God's sake, he'd known her less than an hour. But despite himself he felt a sunburst of lust, instantly overshadowed by guilt. You were supposed to be favourably inclined towards the naturalness of nursing mothers yet always remain sexually detached. But he felt swamped by intense sensations, conflicted on several levels and, basically, like a pimply fourteen-year-old again. Something in his being had shifted. He tried to focus on her scar.

'Dad was good with animals,' China Mason said, very calmly, as she burped the baby on her shoulder. 'Kind, not the shooting sort – not even rabbits. He could handle reptiles, no worries. He could get possums out of the ceiling without a scratch on him.' Ten years later, she went on, she was working behind the bar in a Newcastle hotel when he walked in. 'That was a shock. He saw me, too, downed his beer and walked out. I didn't run after him. If that was his attitude, bugger him.'

'*Whew!*' Genuinely moved, he was still trying to meet her eyes, and succeeded.

'At least I inherited the animal thing from him,' said China Mason. 'The lifelong interest.'

'Yes.'

'I see you're wondering about my scar?'

'Not at all,' he lied.

'Acid,' she said.

'Oh.'

His unasked question hung burning in the air. She didn't elaborate, but finished the breast-feeding then. What passion must she have aroused to cause the acid attack – and what sort of jealous, evil bastard would do that to her? To Leon K., the time it took her to adjust her clothing, burp the baby again and place her in the carry-cot flew by incredibly fast. His brain raced with possible delaying tactics, but he could hardly offer her a drink this early in the morning, or round up more suffering wildlife. 'Ayeshia doesn't much resemble me, does she?' she remarked absently. 'All that blonde hair. She takes after my ex-partner.'

Why did he feel elated at that little prefix, the simple *ex-*?

And at her bringing it to his attention? His gratitude extended far beyond her ridding him of the snake. It stretched all the distance over different years and landscapes to the scar on her cheek. She was becoming more attractive and mysterious by the second, the scar adding vulnerability to her sensual intrigue. Not to mention the lyrebird tattoo on her hip and her hair like dark cascading water.

It dawned on him suddenly that he could easily embarrass her, and himself, with an inappropriate outpouring of enthusiasm. With wild compliments and avid interest. She'd think him mad and creepy. Actually, he did wonder if he'd become completely stir-crazy lately and he was glad it was too early in the day for him to be anything but sober. Really, he should watch himself in company, especially in female company. He walked her sensibly to her van. There was a danger his feelings might show in his tight facial expression; he realised his emotions were in a precarious state but he still had some self-restraint and dignity left, and all he ended up saying to her was, 'How much do I owe you?'

She gave him her card. As well as her name and contact number, it said: *We volunteers gratefully accept what you think is a reasonable donation towards saving our wildlife.* Her eyes widened at the reckless cheque he pressed into her hands, an amount certain to perplex the investigative auditors in days to come. 'Seriously? Are you sure? Wow! Thank you!' She sounded like a teenager just handed prized concert tickets. 'Call us if you have any more creature problems,' said China Mason, Wildlife Saviour, tooting the horn and waving blithely as she drove off through the tunnel of camphor laurels and down the driveway.

For perhaps half an hour Leon K. sat in a patch of sun on the veranda steps, considering a cloud of gnats hanging over the pool. Vibrating, thousands of tiny wings beating in unison. Beyond the tiers of camphor laurels and over the cane fields, a thin stripe of sea stretched in a north–south rectangle between the headlands. The vista of parallel pale blues and greens was like the flag of some temperate northern country. Birds called, the filter-box lid tap-tapped, and eventually the hovering gnat mass moved on.

So he was able to swim again – but with the obstacle removed, there seemed to be less urgency. Eventually he stood anyway, stepped out of his clothes and walked to the pool, swinging his arms to loosen up after the enforced lay-off. He dived in, turned on to his back underwater and began stroking. Striving to appreciate the streaming clouds as usual, the skittering swifts, the pelicans soaring high today over the cane fields, he swam one lap, two . . . It took three laps before the waves and backwash from his progress agitated the filter box enough for the snake to curl out from the air-space between the filter and the pool's surface.

Desperate to escape the pool, a red-bellied black, longer and sleeker than the original – or maybe this one *was* the original – slid up his torso, rode his panicking body to the edge and escaped into the palms. As China Mason had pointed out, black snakes, though venomous, are relatively timid. A measure of its anxiety was that it bit Leon K.'s neck on its way to freedom.

He got inside to the telephone, even found her Wildlife Saviours card in his trouser pocket. Her number rang and rang but finally she answered. Water was puddling the carpet and a thin stream of watered blood dripped pink from his neck and down his chest. Already his throat was constricting. Finally she answered.

'What do I do now?' Leon K. asked her. Repeatedly. 'What do I do now?' He pictured her face. His voice was dry and already disappearing, so he had to hurry. 'I'm sorry,' he apologised. 'I'm not from here.'

The Obituary of Gina Lavelle

WHILE CROCODILES LEAPT out of the muddy African river and grabbed river-fording wildebeests by the snout, Clare Wolfe read the morning paper. She set the exercise bike's controls for thirty minutes on the cardio setting – hills of varying steepness alternating with plateaus and valleys – which was generally the time it took her to read the newspaper end to end. Not sport, finance or the classifieds, but everything else. If she wasn't diverted while she pedalled, her body announced it was exhausted after only five minutes. But if she was engrossed in something, anything other than the compilation of animal maulings and flamboyant human bloopers on the gym's TV, her legs and lungs seemed oblivious to the exertion and she could pedal to the time limit.

Her forty-eighth birthday was approaching and weight-loss hints had been made at home. More than hints – Gavin had been surprisingly hurtful, especially since he'd never looked trimmer himself. She'd decided it was time to join a gym. Secretly. She liked the idea, a few months down the track, of surprising him with a svelte new HealthWorks body.

The floor exercises and weights were still a novelty and diverting in a heavy, repetitive sort of way, but she found stationary cycling so boring that it had taken her a month even to begin to benefit from this supposedly valuable aerobic exercise. HealthWorks was on the first floor, above a hair-removal clinic, discount book warehouse and Oodles of Noodles, and the exercise bikes and StairMasters were lined up along the plate-glass window overlooking Pier Street. There was a wide view of the river.

On the first few visits it had been interesting enough while she pedalled to gaze at the Johnson River streaming one way or the other below her. Although crocodile- and wildebeest-free, it was quite scenic if you disregarded the fort-like public toilet dominating the near bank and focused instead on the far, mangrove-covered shore. For an estuary its currents were also extraordinarily fast-flowing. Only three weeks ago, reddened by ten days of heavy rain from the trailing edge of Cyclone Laura, it had briefly resembled that muddy African river on the TV, and she'd watched fallen trees, a cane chaise longue and a bloated sheep speed past on their way to the river mouth and then, tiny specks, bump over the bar and out into the Pacific.

But apart from sport-fishing boats and the weekly Seniors' Coffee Tours on the paddle-steamer *Mississippi Gambler*, it wasn't normally a busy river, and the view of distant mangroves and emerging or disappearing sandbanks, a rusted dredge, the usual two or three elderly breakwater fishermen, a scattering of gulls, pelicans and cormorants, and of course the toilet edifice, quickly palled. After only a few minutes of pedalling she was bored and puffing.

So Clare tried the diversion of the TV on which Darren Ho, the gym proprietor, continually ran his compilations of race-car crashes, skiing accidents, bungee-jump miscalculations, zebra-seeking lionesses, wedding-day mishaps (tipsy mother-of-the-bride falls into cake; nervous groom projectile vomits over priest) and her least favourite – the crocs surging out of the river into the migrating wildebeest herd. For a muscle man with exaggeratedly huge shoulders and pectorals, Darren was quite mild-mannered, although Clare found his shaved legs and armpits almost as disconcerting as his taste in entertainment. There was something about sporting accidents, and harmless animals being torn apart by predators, that sat uneasily with the purpose of the gym. They made her too anxious to keep pedalling. The marriage mishaps were wearing a bit thin, too.

The street scene below had also failed as an exercise diversion. Apparently, drunken fights and vandalism were rife when the midnight crowds spilled out of the pubs, but not much happened in daytime Pier Street. As she pedalled she'd sometimes guess which passers-by were heading for the full body wax, which ones for a remaindered airport novel or Thai takeaway. From their general age, shape and clothing, however, and their propensity for electric oldster-buggies ostentatiously trailing two or even three Australian flags, not many of them ever seemed candidates for these experiences. In any case, the street scene also only accounted for a few minutes' pedalling.

But the newspaper distraction worked well. The minutes

and mock-kilometres flew by. Two birds with one stone – she was up to date these days on politics, celebrity misdemeanours, Third World earthquakes, fine dining, the trend towards olive growing, suicide bombing and most of the current wars. On the day in question, however, the paper seemed slimmer, the world a calmer place than usual. Fifteen minutes into her exercise routine and she'd nearly finished reading. Only the obituaries stood between her and the weather, comics and horoscopes. On the page before her was a photograph of a glamorously haughty, early-1960s-era blonde entering a courthouse besieged by press reporters and cameramen. The heading said *The Complete Goodtime Girl*. Clare began reading the obituary of a woman called Gina Lavelle.

The name rang no bells. *Gina Lavelle*, she read, *was by turns a Las Vegas showgirl, B-movie actress, gangster's moll, perjurer, stripper and memoirist*. Intrigued, Clare kept reading, and pedalled on. *Born Ruby-Ann Dulch to deeply religious Baptist parents in San Marcos, Texas, she was convicted of perjury in 1960 when her boyfriend, the racketeer Giuseppe 'Joey the Nose' Goldman, was tried for tax evasion. Her year in gaol was fatal to her nascent Hollywood career.*

Clare looked up from the page for a moment to wipe her damp forehead. On the screen above her a racing car lost a wheel, skittered off the track, bounced, rolled, burst into flames and segued into two lionesses, working ruthlessly in tandem, stalking a zebra foal. Below her, perhaps a hundred metres east down Pier Street, an off-white Toyota Prado was backing into a space by the breakwater. Clare turned back to the obituary. *Ruby-Ann ran away from home at fifteen to enter and win a Marilyn Monroe look-alike contest, and became a super-size bra model and Las Vegas showgirl. By the age of eighteen, she had married twice and had two children.*

From the exercise bike she couldn't see the Prado's licence plate but it was a common model, as was the colour, and most of them had that type of roof-rack. She kept up her pedalling rate. Little red electronic numbers told her eighty calories and three kilometres had gone. Eighty calories was just a small apple, or half a cappuccino. On-screen, a bungee-jumper's shocked friends were stammering that they couldn't understand how the accident had happened when Troy had made the same jump from the top of Victoria Falls three times before, and in the wet season. One thing they agreed on was that he would've wanted to go that way. Clare refocused and read: *An inveterate attention-seeker, Gina Lavelle came to public notice when her regular nightclub antics earned her a four-page spread in* Life *magazine. Later, working as a highly paid stripper, she was romantically involved with Albert Anastasia, head of the so-called Murder, Inc.*

On Clare pedalled. The priest on-screen silently mouthed, 'Do you take this woman . . .' and, in anticipation, Clare managed to avert her face as, once more, the young groom, ashen and sickly, vomited over the priest's robes. As always, the bride's face was a picture. A hundred calories gone, twenty minutes, four kilometres. Down the end of Pier Street, sitting previously unnoticed on the breakwater, a dark-haired woman slowly stood up just then, brushed back her hair and strolled, smiling, towards the Prado. The southerly breeze gusting across the river ruffled her billowy skirt. Gulls hung in the air above her. Choppy waves snapped against the breakwater. Clare couldn't make out the woman's face but her body was slender and Clare somehow knew she was attractive.

A man got out of the Prado and faced the dark-haired woman, but he made no move towards her. He stayed close to the car, his back to the street, standing perfectly still, as if watching her intently as she approached him, as if (Clare imagined) he was appreciating the sight of her. Drinking her in. When the woman reached him, she moved into his arms and they kissed and held each other for a long moment. His back was still to Clare. Did he have a small bald spot? What sort of jacket was he wearing? Obstacles were in the way – the street verge of oleander bushes with pink flowers, litter bins, telephone poles, gulls hovering low in the wind, pedestrians – and it was hard to make out anything more.

The man and woman got into the car and the Prado pulled out from the kerb and accelerated away. In Africa, the zebra herd grazed upwind. Camouflaged in the veldt grass, the lionesses crouched low and inched forward on their bellies. In close-up you could see flies crawling on the lions' faces, in their eyes and lips. They paid no attention.

The obituary of Gina Lavelle, nee Ruby-Ann Dulch, said her memoir, *All Woman*, boasted of affairs with more than 2000 men, including several US senators, three FBI investigators, Joe DiMaggio, Howard Hughes, Johnny Weissmuller, Cary Grant, Frank Sinatra and John Wayne. Her claims to have been President John F. Kennedy's lover when he was still a college boy had never been proven. But the way Gina Lavelle stared so languidly from the photograph, Clare could believe anything of her, and nothing.

She was pedalling faster now, and the machine was vibrating so much the newspaper slid to the floor. She pedalled even faster, traversing a continent, a Grand Canyon, of illuminated rectangular highlands, gorges and buttes. Without lessening speed she reached her preset half-hour and flashing red letters on a dashboard above the handlebars beeped congratulations to her, saying *High Five!* and *Cool Down Now!* She pedalled on. The whole electronic landscape fell away behind her, the hills and valleys now flatlined and defeated. But she kept pedalling, even through the growing discomfort in her chest. For the life of her, as long as she could still breathe, Clare Wolfe couldn't imagine ever stopping.

Sea Level

IT WAS BARELY two hours since they'd dropped off their children at school that morning but parents suddenly began arriving to collect them. Jasmine's mother tore into the classroom, grabbed Jasmine's hand and tried to tug her outside. Jasmine was only six and Special Needs and her reaction was especially bewildered and noisy. Jasmine's mother was wildly floundering somewhere between sign language and spoken words as she panicked Jasmine out the door. Mrs Morris's expression showed she wished Jasmine's mother hadn't been so flushed and dramatic.

Then Ben's father burst in, still in his hat and farm boots, sweating anxiously and smelling of fertiliser. He'd left the motor running in the truck. As he shuffled and stamped self-consciously in the doorway, his boots dropped little clumps of red dirt. He looked from Mrs Morris to the other children and back again, apologetically, as if he wished things were different. 'Come on, mate,' he said eventually, and snatched his son's hand.

Then Lily's mother arrived, half dressed and hectic, her navel ring and one wing of her butterfly tattoo showing, and started repeating the morning's radio bulletins in a frenetic way. 'This is sea level!' she stated emphatically to no one in particular. Mrs Morris gave Lily's mother a frown, and made a lip-zipping gesture. In a strangled sort of voice, Mrs Morris announced, 'Everything's under control here, Lily's mother.' Lily started gathering up her books and pencils, but her mother said, 'God, don't worry about those!' and rushed her off without them.

Other parents came and left quickly with their children. Between the arrivals and departures, Max noticed, Mrs Morris kept sneaking glances out the window. But apart from all the cars pulling up and speeding off, there was nothing different to see out there. Lots of flat land. The playground.

Ocean Beach Road. Some sort of big bird, a pelican, high in the sky. A plume of smoke from a cane fire. Then tall pine trees, the tip of the lighthouse showing above them, the rocky point, a flat ribbon of blue ocean and, far out at sea, one little white boat like a drawing.

This was a small school in a fishing and sugarcane village not quite on the tourist track – thirty-three children, two classrooms of composite classes – and soon there was only Sylvie from Year Three and Max left. Sylvie was a year ahead of Max, and a lot taller, with pierced ears and a grown-up hairstyle, but Max thought she looked about to cry.

Mr Lyndon came into the room then and murmured something behind his hand to Mrs Morris. Mrs Morris nodded. The principal cleared his throat and rattled his keys and loose change in his pockets and stood up on his toes and down again. 'Morning, guys,' he said, his manner even jollier than usual, his hair spikier, his cheeks pinker, his movements jerkier. 'Nothing to worry about here. You two can eat your lunches now, if you like.'

It felt far too early to eat their lunches and Max wasn't hungry anyway. Then, as if they weren't there, Mr Lyndon asked Mrs Morris, 'Is your car out the front, Ingrid?' Mrs Morris was taller and older than Mr Lyndon. She said, 'Yes, Don,' and she looked out the window again towards the sea.

'Well,' said Mr Lyndon, and gave a sort of coughing laugh. 'I'd say this was the perfect opportunity to learn about tsunamis.' He moved to the blackboard and drew a rough map of Australia, then chalked in a few little blobs to the north-east. 'The Solomon Islands,' he said. 'Main products: fish, timber, palm oil and coconuts.' He drew a shape like an explosive-looking sun nearby. 'Big earthquake in the Pacific Ocean,' he said. He drew little quivery lines radiating out from it towards Australia, growing bigger, and sharper, like lightning bolts, as they approached the east coast. 'It caused this big wave,' said Mr Lyndon, and drew a recognisable but not hugely threatening wave. 'We call this a tsunami. When one of these fellows hits the shore it can sometimes cause a heap of damage.'

Mrs Morris pinched her mouth shut and stared over Max's and Sylvie's heads at the posters of *Our Nearest Neighbours and the Foods They Eat* pinned to the back of the room, as if she were deliberately refraining from looking out the window.

SEA LEVEL

'Who remembers seeing that big tsunami on TV a couple of years ago?' asked Mr Lyndon. 'No? Anyway, that's why we have a clever warning system that tells us if a tsunami is on the way.'

Sylvie started crying then and Mrs Morris produced a tissue box and handed her a tissue. 'Where's Mum?' sobbed Sylvie. 'Everything's OK,' said Mrs Morris. 'There's no need for her to come and get you. If a big wave came, we'd look after you. That's our job. One of our jobs.'

'What does the warning system tell us?' asked Mr Lyndon. 'Anyone know? It tells us to stay off the beach and not to go surfing or swimming or fishing until the danger is over.'

'And to go to high ground,' murmured Mrs Morris, glancing quickly out the window again, and then to the fish, rice, yams and coconuts of the *Nearest Neighbours* on the back wall.

'Obviously, Ingrid,' muttered Mr Lyndon.

A car pulled up outside then, its door slammed, rubber soles squeaked on the wooden floor, and Sylvie's mother ran in looking flustered, in her tennis dress. 'Here she is,' said Mrs Morris, frowning. 'Good old Mum.' Max noticed that

Mrs Morris's face, too, was pinker than usual. In a matter of seconds the car was accelerating away.

Max sat there at his desk, alone with his teacher and the principal. 'Max, my boy,' said Mr Lyndon, his roaming eyes finally having no choice but to settle on him. 'Mighty Maxie.' He cleared his throat again and looked interested. 'Are you playing football this season?'

Max shrugged. It was still summer. Football was in winter. He never thought about football.

'You've got a fair turn of speed, I've noticed,' said Mr Lyndon, nodding approvingly. 'The league scouts will be after you, if you keep it up. Right, Ingrid?'

Mrs Morris's face flickered, grimaced, then settled back into a frown.

Max shrugged again. Mr Lyndon's mobile phone rang just then. 'Excuse me,' he said. He flourished the phone dramatically before answering it, listened a moment and began to smile. 'Thank you,' he said into the phone. '*Grazie, merci, danke schön.*'

Mr Lyndon looked as if he were about to dance or burst into song. 'Well, well,' he said. 'Tsunami warning cancelled.

No tidal waves. Not even a ripple. How about that?'

'I thought as much,' said Mrs Morris.

Max stared out the window at the distant strip of flat sea. The white boat had gone. The tip of the lighthouse still gleamed in the sun. The playground was strangely silent and bare. He felt dazed and not entirely himself, more like the Max in a dream.

The teachers were looking at him in a different way, with strange smiles, as if he had more importance than usual, as if he had a rare disease and his hair had fallen out and they were visiting him in hospital. His unique status almost overwhelmed him. The boy for whom no one came.

The Water Person and the Tree Person

FOR SOME REASON, Andy Melrose's
started describing him in company as a
haps this could sound summery and s
vaguely sensual, but he wasn't sure s
not after twenty-three years. No d
cally because she would add, r
a bush person'. Or sometime
thought, rather preciously),

Was she just saying the
like cat people and dog
codes? Or was she maki
entious and environ

that by comparison he was a shallow hedonist?
was suddenly implying something seriously
natures. Or, perversely, wishing it to be
that she was setting him up as the
w territory, habits, hobbies
in that wasn't neces-
he seemed to be

the sea,
What's
arri',
cu-
ther
timb

THE WATER PERSON AND THE TREE PERSON

He reminded Lynne that he'd signed petitions to save rainforests in Brazil and Malaysia and old-growth forests in Tasmania. He'd declined doing ads for companies associated with woodchipping or pulp mills. And, he felt bound to stress, he had a tree bias; he felt more favourably inclined towards gum trees than, say, old-world oaks or larches or ashes. Indeed, the time he felt most nationalistically *Australian*, most serenely in tune with his continent, was when he rounded a coastal bush track and glimpsed the summer surf glistening through a canopy of eucalypts.

What did she expect? Unlike her, he'd grown up on this limestone coast, with the roaring forties blowing sand into his ears and the smell of estuary algae in his nostrils every night as he fell asleep. Ever since, the landscape in his mind's eye was a crumbly moonscape of a coastline, a glaring bleached desert fringed by those two big and wondrous oases, the Swan River and the Indian Ocean.

His psyche preferred a view of water, but he didn't see why it was necessary for their relationship that he state a 100 per cent preference for coast or bush. Lynne, the product of a middle-class Melbourne garden suburb of autumnal tones and spring blossoms and the manicured cold-weather flora of Europe, seemed almost political about it, as though his personal and cultural integrity depended on a firm commitment to landscape. It was as if he had to come out for either the dingo or the shark, but not both.

All his life he'd surfed, sailed and swum, but he thought he liked the bush well enough – as long as the ocean was in striking distance or there was a glimmer of river or lake nearby. In any case, despite Lynne's avowed vote for the outback, it was she who made the bookings for their annual summer holidays, and always chose the coast.

In twenty-three years she'd never suggested a bushwalking, camping or farm-stay holiday. For that matter, it was difficult to imagine his wife on a horse, or hiking, or in the vicinity of cowpats. He couldn't picture her sitting in a tent, or drinking billy tea, or picking burrs out of her socks, much less cauterising leech bites or humping a knapsack through a gravelly landscape of banksias and tiger snakes.

Sometimes he wondered whether her constantly declared love for the bush was just literary-political correctness, a more culturally sound position for an academic and book reviewer, just like her preference for Australian literature set in the past. All those stories of shallow handsome graziers, feisty plain women and earthy farm labourers with sinewy forearms left him cold. They reminded him of opera without the fat people or the singing. As for their prickly understated romances under the jacarandas, he'd grumble, 'I never know if they're having sex or not.'

Give him an American crime novel with lots of forensics any day. A cannibal serial killer? Why not? But then he was just an ad-man, with the tastes of the hoi polloi.

It was after one of their dinner parties, when she'd produced her first edition of *Kangaroo*, D.H. Lawrence's take on Australia's political landscape in the '20s, that he realised how seriously she took this topographical schism between them. 'Listen,' she said to the table, the guests mostly people from her department, 'I was re-reading this the other day, and it struck me that Richard Somers could be Andy. It's absolutely Andy! He could be Lawrence's character, or rather Lawrence himself. This is exactly how Andy thinks of the bush.'

Chuckles all round. And of course she then read two or

three pages about Lawrence's terror of the West Australian bush. *It was so phantom-like, so ghostly, with its tall pale trees and many dead trees, like corpses, partly charred by bush fires: and then the foliage so dark, like grey-green iron. And then it was so deathly still. Even the few birds seemed to be swamped in silence. Waiting, waiting – the bush seemed to be hoarily waiting. And he could not penetrate into its secret. He couldn't get at it. Nobody could get at it. What was it waiting for?*

They were all smiling at him across their wine glasses. As if this wasn't at all a new topic of conversation for them. Not quite smirking – he was their host, after all, the husband of their colleague – but with a sort of joint comfort in the value of their scholarship (proven once again!) versus his commercial success. (Advertising, no less!) And another sort of wheezy self-regard as well. A smugness in their fogeyish physical deterioration, their deliberate lack of style (cold-weather clothing in all seasons), their indoor-ness, their proud ineptitude with cars and computers and technology in general. From their barely masked sneers when he'd let slip that he went swimming most days, had had to change a flat tyre that morning, and was trying, against the odds, to stay

THE WATER PERSON AND THE TREE PERSON

in shape, you'd think he'd been confessing to steroids and testosterone injections.

And then Lynne was reading again. *One night at the time of the full moon he walked alone into the bush . . . he walked on, had walked a mile or so into the bush, and had just come to a clump of tall, nude, dead trees, shining almost phosphorescent with the moon, when the terror of the bush overcame him . . . There was a presence . . .*

'It sounds exciting,' he'd said. 'My sort of book.' But he was hurt and mystified by her mockery. 'Of course, she's right about Lawrence and me,' he joked. 'We agree on most things. Never trust the gardener, for a start.' Where did she get this view of him? Anyway, how often did these flabby litterateurs get out into the bush? Had they ever been ten kilometres out of town?

In any case, this year he and Lynne were holidaying on the south-west coast as usual, in late January as always, when the crowds were drifting back to the cities, and at Figtree Inlet again. Indeed, in the same cottage among the gums with its wide veranda view of the river mouth and the Indian Ocean surf beyond that they'd rented – that

Lynne had initiated and organised – for the past eleven or twelve summers.

There was one difference: this year for the first time he wasn't spending every day in the surf. After a lifetime of surfing, his knees had finally given up on squatting and swivelling. Arthritis had teased and twinged and now painfully settled. Not that he'd surrendered without a struggle. He'd attempted to delay the inevitable by swapping a shortboard's wave-ripping and carving possibilities for that stolid stand-by of the middle-aged surfer, the Malibu. But even on the longboard his knees ached, followed by aches in his ankles and lower back. He might as well sign up for the age pension; to Andy Melrose it seemed like the beginning of the end.

In the circumstances, Lynne's Christmas gift had come as a pleasurable surprise. With a modest fanfare, and a lot of wrapping paper, she'd presented him with a kayak. Not only was it a thoughtful gift, it was clearly way beyond the price range of her usual presents: the crime novels or sporting biographies or Dylan CDs. Andy Melrose was touched and grateful.

Obviously she was acknowledging that their recent

emotional impasse was over and she was offering him a new physical – and watery – interest to battle his middle-aged melancholy. He thanked God that the tree person and the water person weren't becoming remote strangers, after all. He understood that the kayak, a handsome four-metre, mango-coloured craft called a Nemo – equally suited to stream, river, lake or ocean – was a token of her love and understanding.

Rather than launch the Nemo in the Swan River, his hectic home waters, battling the ferries and yachts and millionaires' pleasure boats, he'd saved up its first outing for a month, until their own holidays. And now on this mid-afternoon in late January, the summer hubbub at Figtree Inlet nearly over and most of the estuary's other craft either moored for the season or on their way back to the suburbs in trailers or on car roof-racks, he intended to take it out for its test-run.

Australia Day had come and gone the day before. On the public holiday he and Lynne had watched from the veranda as some skylarking youths on surf-skis paddled out a kilometre or so to a small sand island in the middle of the estuary. There, in mock ceremony, they planted the Australian flag, saluted it and toasted it with beer.

Andy Melrose had envied them their gesture. He'd always wanted to paddle out there, stand on the sand and claim the island himself. 'I'm going to do that tomorrow,' he'd announced to Lynne.

Twice a day this little elongated island rose from the water and bisected the Melroses' view, the sandbank never quite the same shape or surfacing in the same spot. From the veranda it was pale and flat, some days resembling an ice floe, on others more like a desert island in a cartoon; all it lacked was a coconut palm and a castaway.

Setting out, Andy Melrose hadn't felt this enthusiastic about anything for years. As he strained to lift the Nemo on to the car roof, he joked to Lynne that it was true what they said about kayaking: 'The main exercise comes from lifting the kayak on and off the car.'

'Enjoy yourself,' she said. Driving away from the holiday house, he was already eagerly anticipating his heroic, manly wave to her from the island. In a way, waving to her and receiving her returning wave was the whole romantic point, even after twenty-three years. Maybe because of the twenty-three years.

THE WATER PERSON AND THE TREE PERSON

He launched the kayak from the fig-tree flats on the eastern side of the estuary and pointed the bow towards the island. Well, it floated. And it supported him. It didn't tip, as he'd feared, and it powered through the water. From the first dip of the paddle, he found the Nemo exhilarating. The effort was all in the buttocks and shoulders; once they'd adjusted to the roll and rhythm his spirits rose even further. The sensation was quite different to sitting in a boat. In an ordinary boat you were above the water, separated from it, whereas the Nemo made him feel part of the estuary's surface. Like a floating, bobbing seabird, his undercarriage was attuned and reactive to every ripple.

Kayaking, he discovered, was a mental as well as a physical exercise. By the time he reached the sandbank he felt rigorously tested, but mentally invigorated and strangely serene. Of course he was satisfied with himself for being so intrepid. Knowing he was being watched (and even applauded) from afar only intensified the pleasure. He felt as proud and youthful as a boy showing off on his first bicycle. *Look, Mum. No hands!*

He found it was impossible to simply stand up and step

out of the kayak; he had to roll over rather ponderously until the kayak tipped him out on his side into the muddy shallows. Laughing at himself, he thought, *that'll amuse Lynne.* But he wouldn't try to catch her eye just yet; he was waiting for the proper moment. Dripping with mud and reeds, panting, his knees and lower back playing up again, he lurched in several clumsy stages to his feet.

The sand was unexpectedly marshy; the tide was coming in. Fighting suction, sinking knee-deep in the ooze, Andy Melrose valiantly faced the shore. The water was rushing over the sandbank now and the wind was biting through his wet clothes. The sun was behind the headland. He had better hurry. Against the tide and wind, paddling back would be hard-going.

The only sound on the whole empty estuary was the urgent lapping of the incoming tide on the sandbank. The afternoon light was fading but eventually he picked out the cottage. Dwarfed by the thick surrounding eucalypts, the tall gums, it looked tiny and strangely deserted from here, as one-dimensional and insubstantial as a film set. Now was his moment. He waved his arms vigorously. *Lynne, I made it!*

THE WATER PERSON AND THE TREE PERSON

The veranda was bare. He stared more intently but there was no one to be seen. How could this be? The cottage was a faded, Depression-era timber bungalow and it looked as if it hadn't seen paint or human habitation for decades. Behind and all around the cottage, the bush loomed back at him.

The Whale Watchers

THE LAST TIME Tom ever saw his father, the humpbacks were migrating north from the Antarctic to spend the winter in warmer Queensland waters. Tom thought whale watching seemed a safe proposition – otherwise his father and Sonia were just self-consciously hanging around the house, exclaiming at the bird life and picking up magazines and putting them down again. The trouble with living on the north coast was that southerners felt bound to include you and your spare room in their holiday plans. Even their honeymoon plans, in the case of his father and his bride.

Until he received the wedding invitation Tom hadn't even known his father had a girlfriend. His father was a quantity surveyor, widowed not quite two years, and hitting sixty; Sonia was a divorced allergy-products salesperson, forty-fiveish, Tom guessed. They'd met in Bali the year before while getting over their separate sorrows around the pool bar at The Oberoi. After three days' in-house observation of the new couple, with four still to go, Tom found it hard to imagine his stepmother being depressed in Bali or anywhere else. Sonia was a vivacious and decorative person. Even her asthma and migraine hadn't kept her down for long, and she'd smiled through both attacks those first two days.

The honeymoon was difficult for Tom to get his head around. He didn't know if he and Chloe should be trying to entertain the older couple or allowing them complete privacy. In their presence he felt strangely impatient and crotchety, as if his and his father's ages and roles had been reversed. At breakfast he feigned hostly heartiness, poured orange juice and didn't know where to look, just as his father had behaved with him and his overnight girlfriends when he was twenty. At night he heard them murmuring as he was preparing for bed but, thankfully, the spare room was at the far end of the house and he was able to block out the possibility of any intimate noises with a series of closed doors. That side of things didn't bear thinking about.

'I think they're cute,' said Chloe.

'He's not your parent,' Tom replied. Anyway, his father and Sonia were 'just driving through' on their way north to Port Douglas, heading for two weeks on the Great Barrier Reef and, presumably, as much privacy as they wanted.

Before whale watching, Tom suggested lunch at a beachside cafe, The Undertow. It was full of young backpackers sharing pasta in various accents, admiring their new tans and repeatedly counting out their money in heaps on the table. 'Isn't this younger generation growing much taller than us oldies?' Sonia said loudly. 'It doesn't matter which country they're from, even the Asians, they make me feel like a midget.'

'What nonsense,' said Chloe. 'What are you – five-nine?'

'Five-nine and a half,' said Sonia. 'The same as my hubby.' She fondly patted his bald patch.

'He's five-eight,' said Tom. 'Unless he's grown since I was a boy.'

'Let's order, shall we?' his father said. He squinted at the name badge on the waitress's breast. He'd left his glasses behind. 'What do you recommend, Stephanie?'

'Shoshani,' said the waitress. 'It's all on the board. Calamari's off.'

Over lunch, Sonia loudly admired the artwork on the cafe walls – amateur representations of sunsets, dawns and rainbows over Mount Warning – busily took note of the artists' names on a napkin, and only nibbled at her prawn salad. Before Tom and Chloe had finished eating, his father already had his wallet out, waving away any opposition, but then landed in a credit-card disagreement. As Shoshani kept saying, the cafe accepted only Visa and Mastercard.

'Shoeshine, I must say I find that unacceptable,' said his father, waving his platinum Amex. 'Is there anyone in authority I can speak to?' Sipping the dregs of her mango smoothie, Chloe had a coughing fit then, and she and Tom avoided each other's eyes. Tom ended up settling in cash.

His father was still seething when they reached the Cape and Tom parked the car. They hiked along the steep coastal path to a cliff below the lighthouse. His father and Sonia deliberately fell behind, and when they caught up, his father's mouth was drawn tight and he was breathing heavily through his nose to cover his puffing. He looked a little flushed around the gills. Tom dimly remembered some paternal health warning-sign four or five years before. His mother had insisted on dietary, tobacco and alcohol changes. No one had dreamt she'd go first.

Chloe and he waited until the older couple caught up. Sonia had her arm hooked in his father's. Outdoors, with her flying blonded hair and pink cheeks, she suddenly looked years younger, buoyant and allergy-free, and surprisingly at ease in the elements.

Southerly winds whipped the tussocky grass, buffeted their faces and made everyone's eyes water. The surly Pacific lurched and rolled towards South America and crashed on the rocks below. In the distance a lone feral goat flicked into sight, skittered improbably up the cliff face and disappeared, a mere blink later, before Tom could point it out. He inhaled the misty wind, exhaled, inhaled again and sighed, less deeply this time.

OK, he thought. He touched his father's shoulder. 'What about this, Dad?' he said. 'Impressive or what?'

'Most easterly point in Australia,' his father read from a sign. His eyes sought another sign. 'Do not climb on the railings,' he read aloud. 'Parents, watch your children.'

'Darling, keep a look out for whales,' said Sonia.

'I am. I can't see any,' his father said.

'You've got to keep looking,' Chloe said. 'Look towards the south. Suddenly one pops up unexpectedly. You'll see it breaching or blowing.'

'Possible rock falls. Keep inside the railings,' his father read out in a louder voice. 'As if you wouldn't,' he scoffed. 'If you had a modicum of bloody sense.'

Tom told them to watch out for the rare white humpback known as Migaloo that appeared off the coast every year. 'Wouldn't you think he'd be called Moby Dick?' he muttered into the wind, to no one in particular.

'Who'd go outside the railings anyway?' his father said. 'Only the Jap tourists, taking their bloody snaps. You'd be asking for trouble. Slippage, rock-falls . . .' He gripped a nearby railing and attempted to shake it. It moved perhaps a millimetre. 'None of this looks too stable, if you want my professional opinion.'

'Why would you name a whale after a restaurant?' mused Sonia. She beamed. 'Just asking. Have you been to Moby

Dick's? Nice seafood but fairly pricey.'

His father was shaking his head in wonderment. 'Wouldn't you think some bright spark would have cottoned on to printing the signs in Japanese?'

They all huddled together on the cliff as the southerly gusted into their faces. For a long moment no one spoke. '*Brr!*' shivered Sonia. 'Come on, you whales!' she called brightly, like a soccer mother urging on her child's team. She jogged on the spot for a moment to get warm, then reached out and smoothed Tom's wind-ruffled hair with both hands. She patted his shoulder. 'There you go, stepson.'

'Thank you, wicked stepmother,' he said.

'Better keep your eyes on the sea, or we'll miss them,' said Chloe.

'When you two have finished larking about, we might get on with the business at hand,' his father said, pointing at a foamy chasm below. 'I saw something big just then and you two missed it.'

'They don't come that close into shore,' Tom said.

'Probably a dolphin,' said Chloe. 'This is a popular spot for dolphins.'

'I saw a dorsal fin. Could be a shark,' his father said. 'It'd make it worthwhile if it was a shark.'

Sonia asked then, 'Darling, did you look like Tom when you were young? Dark-haired and wiry?'

'What? I don't know. Probably.' He frowned, and jerked his coat collar around his chin. 'Yes, I did. Back when I was six-foot-two. Why do you ask?'

'Just wondering.'

'They're very alike,' Chloe said. 'Your chap and mine.'

'Mum always used to say that,' said Tom.

His father pulled his collar higher against the wind. His jacket looked new, a fashion choice for a younger, hipper, perhaps bigger man. The shoulders slightly overhung his own. 'I think we'd better head off a bit earlier than we thought,' he said. 'We'll make tracks and hit the highway this afternoon. I'd like to make Brisbane before tonight.'

Sonia looked slightly surprised. 'He doesn't like driving at night anymore,' she said.

'Look!' said Tom, suddenly pointing out into the bay. 'There's a whale!'

'There's whales where we're going,' said his father.

Stones Like Hearts

EVERYONE IMAGINES THE shore of Shelly Beach to be covered in, well, shells. There are plenty of shells but what strikes the visitor – especially after those savage winter storms off Cape Leeuwin, where the Indian and Southern oceans collide in a maelstrom of tides, spindrift and stinging winds – is the number of stones heaped in glistening, ever-shifting piles on the shore.

Rattling like castanets in the waves, the stones have a powerful appeal to shoreline browsers. They beg to be handled, stroked like worry beads, even souvenired, although the beachcombers who take them home soon discover that the stones lose their startling green, black or sepia sheen once away from the sea.

One Sunday morning in autumn a woman and her young daughter were at Shelly Beach, ostensibly to look for stones of a particular shape. The little girl, Imogen, collected stones that looked like hearts. Over the millennia most stones on this rugged bay that faces Antarctica in the south and Africa in the west have been weathered into round or ovoid shapes. Heart-shaped stones are a rare find.

To stand a chance of resembling hearts the stones need to have been fractured relatively recently (perhaps only 1000 years ago) and then smoothed by the friction between the waves and the millions of other stones. Nevertheless, at home Imogen already had a collection of sixteen stones that, with a little imagination, could be seen to resemble hearts – either hearts or Mickey Mouse's head. But the real reason her mother, Brigid, had suggested visiting this beach at the bottom edge of the world on a blustery Sunday morning was not to collect unusual stones but to throw her wedding ring into the sea.

The incentive for this drastic plan was that Brigid had found her husband's astrological chart in his bedside drawer. Max paying such avid attention to his horoscope? That wasn't like him. Max was a pragmatic, conservative man: a real estate agent, a keen fisherman, surfer, golfer and earnest weekend beer-drinker. On the few occasions she'd heard him even mention astrology, he called it 'mumbo jumbo'. At the golf club he sometimes sounded off about the 'astral travellers' and 'gurus' and 'hippie charlatans' who had bought up cheap land on the sheer, rocky escarpment of the Cape (land whose potential he'd missed) and built ecologically sensitive houses, powered by sun and wind. Brigid was surprised he even knew his own star sign.

But there in her hands was the evidence: a ten-page personal astrological chart that began with the time and place of his birth, and was full of such arcane detail about his character and habits (even the sleepwalking!) and his romantic and sexual proclivities that she had to lie back on the bed – the marital bed, the imprint of his head still on his pillow – to get her breath back.

The chart was printed and bound in an aquamarine folder and inside the cover, in a wispy New Age font resembling underwater calligraphy, a message said: *To my own Ram, lover of lovers, from your Aquarian mermaid.* Max was an Aries.

Lover of lovers? A blunt Cancer herself, Brigid was soon on the phone to him at work.

He admitted it – shamefacedly at first, then, over the following days, self-consciously defiant. He'd been having an affair for nine months, all the way through Brigid's birthday, and Christmas, and their twenty-second wedding anniversary. The Aquarian mermaid, Aurora (née Tracy), was a Reiki masseuse and astrologer, not unusual jobs in this part of the south-west coast, where 'alternative' occupations were no more remarked upon than being a hairdresser or a school teacher elsewhere.

'She and I are on the same journey,' he told his wife, with tears in his eyes. 'She's opened my mind to deeper things. She's made me grow as a person.'

'Bully for you,' said Brigid. 'About time.' When Max announced he was moving in temporarily with his mother in Busselton 'to take a breather and sort things out', but continued to see the mermaid, Brigid decided after a month that she had no choice but to declare their marriage over. And so this blustery Sunday morning, salt mist in their tangled hair, she was at Shelly Beach with Imogen, their youngest daughter, the same beach where Max had gratefully proposed to her after they'd made gritty love in the dunes twenty-three years before.

It had been a warm summer evening, one of those long West Australian dusks redolent of pungent coastal plants, dried kelp and sun-baked limestone, with an occasional faint whiff from some small dead reptile somewhere back in the dunes.

While their skin dried off, they'd lain there watching the sun set, a red whale sinking in the part of the sea that was the Indian Ocean. An offshore breeze dusted them with sand as fine and clinging as talc, grains that still turned up in all sorts of crevices days later. The easterly picked up and blew spidery tumbleweeds into the other part of the sea that was the Southern Ocean. Afterwards he'd been almost speechless, except to propose to her. It was the first time she'd seen him teary-eyed. And then of course they did it again.

As Brigid deliberated over flinging her ring into the ocean, her nerves were zinging. To follow through or not? What a huge step, she thought. She felt like a character in a book or film, the sort of story that in happier days would have irritated her. It would be an overly dramatic cliché, but part of her felt right about it. This was no phony gesture.

Where was the most suitable spot? It was important to find the right place. She was strangely exhilarated: simultaneously sad, bitter and crazy, and her heart was beating faster at the boldness of it. What a satisfying way of reclaiming pride and self. To hurl your wedding ring into the waves would bring – that word she heard all the time lately – 'closure'.

Wild-haired mother and daughter paddled along the gusty beach, Imogen reaching down into the jangling wet stones, examining and discarding and chattering, Brigid pretending to listen while ceaselessly twisting the ring round her finger. She knew this shoreline, but the winter tides and the ever-moving heaps of stones, humped and quivering like beached sea lions in a nature documentary, had altered its aspect. She was searching for a particular pool in a deep rock crevice; she didn't want the ring to be washed ashore or for anyone to ever find it. This was crucial for its burial. She wanted it to sink under water and stones, for anemones to absorb it into their weed-flesh, for shellfish to envelop it. The ring had to be concreted into the timeless seascape of Shelly Beach.

The south end of the beach ended in a natural barrier of elephantine rocks and here they came across a huddle of weekend strollers and rock fishermen. These people looked morosely agitated, all hunched and muttering around a sodden mound on the shore. Some of the women were leaning on each other for support, their faces turned obliquely away. Someone gave a choking cough, like a retch, and turned aside to spit.

The mound looked like a lump of ambergris, but as they approached it, a piece of rag drifted from it in the ebbing of a wave and a bearded man with a fishing rod shouted roughly at Brigid, 'Keep that kid away!'

The mound was a human body lying face down in the sand and it had been in the sea a long time. The hair was long and matted and trailing weed. The skin was frayed, and pitted like pumice. Bits were missing. From what was left of the clothing, shreds of khaki trousers and one sneaker, and the appearance of the other hugely swollen bare foot, it was a man. His race, age, even his build, were impossible to guess. As she attempted to shield Imogen, Brigid heard someone murmur 'they're usually men, aren't they?' and 'tidal drift' and 'they'll be here in a minute', and just then a police car and an ambulance pulled into the parking area above the beach.

Only with the promise of a treat did Brigid manage to hurry Imogen, agog and protesting, from the beach. In the car she turned on the radio and drove to town with all the windows open so they were too blasted by sound and wind to talk.

At McDonald's an hour later, waiting for her daughter to finish her Happy Meal chicken nuggets (she couldn't face food herself), she glanced absently at her watch and noticed the ring was still on her finger. She was twirling it unconsciously, possessively, rolling it back and forth, back and forth, seeking it with an urgency that surprised her.

The Aquarium at Night

AT NIGHT IN his prison cell he tried to write down the way the sunlight struck their gum trees at dawn. The first rays turned the angophoras' trunks gold or orange, Dyson recalled, then pink a few minutes later. Where the trees had shed branches they formed stumps like amputated limbs, and parrots had gnawed out little caves in the wounded and bleeding wood. As the sun rose over the ridge, the rosellas, lorikeets and parakeets peeped out from their nest holes, like suburban householders cautiously facing the fresh day. These sunlit trees were on a sandstone ridge 17 000 kilometres away and twenty years ago.

He put this down on paper. He remembered the first

light on the rock-oyster leases across the bay. The shadow of the escarpment fell in a dark sheen on the surface and from his bedroom window he'd spot the oyster farmer setting out from the mangroves and then disappearing into the shadow as he punted out to his beds. Some mornings the oysterman had a radio with him, and commercial jingles and the insistent babble of the breakfast announcer carried across the black water.

How old was he back then – twelve, thirteen? Already shedding his boring first name – Preston – for the more exotically sportive Pablo. Scribbling *Pablo Dyson – Association of Surfing Professionals World Champion* all over his schoolbooks, alongside countless doodles of extreme waves and reckless riders based on himself. A skinny, mop-headed grommet leaning out the window to check the morning's wind and weather for the day's surf potential and dreaming of legendary breaks. By 6.15 he'd be on his bike, board under his arm. By 6.30 he'd be over the ridge and in the ocean.

In prison, however, he was unable to set down a single word about the surf. The merest thought of sea, sun and wind made his head throb and his body ache with a homesickness that reached down to the bone. What could be more removed from those vital elements than this place? It was less upsetting, even calming, to concentrate on his old bedroom view high on the ridge. In his attic room he'd had a bold image of himself at that age, defying lightning strikes, sniffing distant bushfires and looking down on birds in flight.

Birds flew beneath him, raucous birds crisscrossing below. Most people only saw birds flying overhead; they rarely saw their wing-engineering in action like he did, the muscles and tendons working to keep them airborne as they streaked by. Obviously he was intrigued by flight and balance, what his one year of university architecture would later teach about the symbiosis of function and aesthetics. Cockatoos, magpies, currawongs, butcher birds, kookaburras: they were leisurely enough for him to see what made them tick. But the parrots' flight apparatus was harder to glimpse. Quicker than his reactive sight, they flashed past so fast they left their colours and screeches streaming in their wake. Radiant reds, greens and blues still striping the air.

Ms Shehabe was right. It was amazing what flooded back once you started writing it down. But memories came in fits and starts. Concentration was a problem. Night was the hardest twelve hours of the twenty-four. Lockdown. But she'd said it was still the best time to write. 'Write what you know. Describe what you remember. Think of one image and the rest will follow.' That was the purpose of the first exercise, Angeline Shehabe said. She provided Home Office writing pads and HB pencils. 'To a writer, a pencil's as good as a computer.'

Write what he knew? Well, he knew tonight's order of events, every night's events, for that matter, even before they happened. First, the banging doors coming closer, footsteps coming closer, the sound of keys. Every cell's music suddenly turned on full clashing volume, everyone's territory of sound trying to deaden every other competing noise. Bash it into submission. And he was maybe trying to read a magazine through this din, write a letter, attempt a crossword.

Despite all this racket, ever since the first class he'd been thinking: *what do I know?* Apart from the many shapes of the ocean and women. The trouble was, the things he didn't want to know drowned out what he knew. The night noise swelling louder. Jangling keys again. Thumping. A Cockney

THE AQUARIUM AT NIGHT

voice shouting down the corridor, 'Hey Frankie, Frank!' 'Yeah, what do you want?' 'Goodnight Frank, *ha ha ha*.' Swearing, bad jokes, hilarity. The slap of flesh. Sounds of sobbing. Keys rattling again. Yells. Another 'accident'? A fight? Grunts. Moans. Abruptly, a rare ten, fifteen, twenty seconds of silence. Then mad Mick O'Hare suddenly jabbering furiously again about a stolen bicycle and a fat whore in Leeds in 1994. Down in G-wing a long lone howl, like a wolf on a snowy mountain. Quiet. Then the howl again, straight out of Alaska. Silence. A trombone blast of a fart nearby. An answering one. Laughter. Mad Mick yelling that the hooker swapped the bike for bad smack. Laughter. A Raleigh mountain bike, ten gears, in mint condition. A yell: 'So, Mick! How did you get to choir practice without your bike?'

What he knew. Well, he knew that most of them in here had something in common beyond being crims. They were young and aimless, with short attention spans. They didn't look at the big picture but took the first pleasant option. Easy gratification won out every time. *Easygoing*, they called aimlessness back home. When and where he grew up, *easygoing* was regarded as a male virtue, one he had in spades.

Dropping out after first-year architecture to go surfing year-round had been no big deal in a place where an easy-going nature and good hand-eye coordination made you a decent bloke. Relaxed Athleticism = Proper Australian Man. Change the accents, give them a tan, put them in T-shirts, and these prisoners could be guys he knew back home. Not the gangs, of course, or the shit-throwing maniac-killers in F- or G-wings, or the zoo animals and rock spiders in isolation, but you could transport B-wing holus-bolus to the Ocean View Hotel at midnight any Friday night. Or vice versa. Maybe *easygoing* was something to think about. One of these days.

Should he bother writing all those thoughts for next Thursday's class? He was sunk right in the middle of *that*, he knew *that*. Six months on remand in a nineteenth-century bluestone prison left over from the days of Dickens and foggy cobblestones and Jack the Ripper, he *knew it* by now. But it wasn't what he *knew*.

This was crazy, but what the prisoners thought he knew — because he was Australian he *must* know — was the low-down, the goods, on *Home and Away* and *Neighbours*.

How could an Australian not be an expert on the prison's two all-time favourite shows? It gave him a strange kudos. Amazingly, the prison hubbub came to a halt when the Australian soaps were on TV. All these English murderers and rapists, bank robbers and arsonists and drug dealers, were serious fans.

That was a surprise, their uncritical enthusiasm; urban British crims yearning for the pragmatic tanned girls, suburban ethics and earnest kitchen-table confabs of Australian TV. What's more, they assumed because the soaps were Australian that this Aussie prisoner, this former world champion surfer (so the rumour mill alleged, and he didn't deny it), not only followed them as avidly as they did, but was many episodes ahead of them in knowledge. Hardly differentiating between fantasy and reality, they associated him with coastal TV characters of the same laconic stamp. Either way, he must know what would happen next: who was divorcing, pregnant, having affairs, abruptly leaving town under a cloud, being killed off – the usual soapie stuff. And they *cared* about those shows. No one took the piss.

Coming on top of the soapie connection and the surfing,

his nationality didn't hurt him, either (like all Australians, to them he was from approved convict stock). There was no class barrier to fret about. That he'd already served six months on remand lent the cachet of a serious felony. It all added up to the fact that Pablo Dyson was OK. To be left alone.

Of course he was enigmatic about his supposed plot knowledge, making only cryptic comments like 'that girl's not what she seems' or 'that bloke's luck's going to run out soon'. When in doubt there was always his stand-by: 'I don't want to spoil it for you, mate.' He didn't admit that back home he'd only ever seen one or two episodes, by accident; that back home only kids and old ladies watched the soaps. Depending on the season and the daylight, he was still out in the surf, on the road, with a woman, or in the pub. The longer he was away from home, however, the further he was away from *Home and Away*. If his trial didn't happen soon (he had to be acquitted!), maybe they'd realise Pablo Dyson's soapie knowledge was running out.

Writing down his memories of parrots sent Dyson into a reverie about colour. The fluorescently red and green king parrots, the elegant pink and grey galahs, the yellow crests of the cockatoos. The luxury of colour. When everything outside was ashen or metallic – asphalt, steel, observation towers, razor-wire, and let's not forget the sky – and everything inside was chipped, heavy-duty institution-cream, any colour seemed over the top. Those voluptuous pink angophoras with their moist dimpled flesh; he'd never thought of trees as womanly before, all heaving breasts and undulating Polynesian hips. Which brought back other memories.

At night he'd endeavour to attract sleep by trying to remember in chronological order the women he'd slept with. His version of counting sheep. When he didn't recall, or had never known, their names – which applied to about half of them – he'd think 'the Maui chick' or 'that short blonde at Whale Beach' or 'those two Swedish backpackers at Broken Head' or 'Hendo's ex-wife' or 'the first ever Brazilian' or 'the mad redhead at Rusty's party'. It was an unwieldy list, and his memory was forever jumping out of sequence with images and places, many of them outdoors or unusual. He was sure he'd forgotten a lot, but by the time he'd counted about 150 he was usually asleep anyway.

Thinking of hips – the shy way she kept tugging at her sweater – Angeline Shehabe seemed self-conscious about hers. Like all the female education-unit staff, she deliberately dressed down. Professionally dowdy was advisable in here, all the skinny young women fattened and flattened under layers of floppy shirts, baggy jumpers and loose jeans. Sexually negated. No make-up on any of them, nothing masking their cold sores and dry lips, the bitten fingernails and weary eyes. Only Angeline Shehabe, the one black teacher, suffered none of these Caucasian blemishes, hopelessly failing to conceal the natural beauty of her cheekbones, the definition of her lips and curves. Neither the enforced drabness nor the depressing environment could hide her spark and beauty. From his seat in the writing class, pencil working busily, Pablo Dyson secretly tried to inhale the odour of her.

Did *she* write about what she knew? She'd let slip only a little personal information: she was a poet and she played the piano. (No rings, though, on those poet's and pianist's slim fingers.) And she was from Sierra Leone originally, wasn't she?

Or somewhere just as bloodthirsty. Dyson thought of coups and machetes and massacres and child soldiers with AK-47s. God knows what terrible stuff she knew. Did she also know that all the straight prisoners in the education cell fancied her? That at least one of them was falling in love with her?

The idea of putting this down on paper was strangely thrilling. He ached to write of his feelings about her. He jotted down some carefully obscure and unidentifiable descriptive words: *skin – smooth, lower lip – pink, laughter – nervous, general manner – flustered kindness, appearance – elegant and striking.* Nothing sexual that would count as an offence. If she reported him, they'd throw him out of the class, and worse. Instead, he safely elaborated on his memories of parrots and gum trees and the dawn view of oyster beds in another hemisphere when he was twelve.

In his mind he saw every tree and rock back on their block. Two vertical acres of Hawkesbury sandstone and high eucalypts. The rocks all sixty million years old in their present formations; before that, sixty million years of weathering down to sand. And before that, another sixty million in the making from sand to rock. So the shire council's geotechnical engineer explained when he tested the ridge's ability to bear a house. The only block with a water view his parents could afford. 'It's two acres of air going cheap on the Central Coast,' his father told the family. 'Above a narrow tidal inlet of Broken Bay. Fingers crossed.' The geotech guy poked rods in the ground, chipped and hammered and took measurements, and finally frowned and said all those rocks visible above ground were floaters and unstable. The devastated look on his father's face. 'But the bedrock will support you all right,' said the engineer. 'That bedrock isn't going anywhere for another sixty million.' This fact cheered them up when the house swayed on its pole foundations in every gale. It was a steep climb, too, 107 stairs, but from three sides you could see the sun and moon glistening on the water.

If his reminiscences bored Angeline – they had the rest of the class bewildered and fidgeting – she listened with the same polite encouragement she gave the others' defiant catalogues of family mayhem and early felonies. Of course she maintained a distance. Everyone knew the rules: no prisoner–teacher contact; the merest brush of a hand against her elbow, the touch of fingers during the passing of a book, was forbidden. There was an emergency button on the wall by her seat, and warders – all mutton-faced, slope-shouldered weight-lifters – patrolled the corridor outside. Anyway, in case of trouble (although this would have been news to her) everyone knew that Oswald was her protector. A twenty-stone Christian who'd decapitated his son-in-law with an axe for infidelity, Oswald had informed them all that he looked on Angeline as a daughter.

Oswald always sat himself next to her, giant African hands resting placidly on the table, his pad and pencils arranged at right angles. As soon as Angeline introduced the lesson, Oswald took up his pencil and began his customary creative endeavour. No matter what she was trying to get across – characterisation, plot, dialogue – he wrote the same first-person sentence in gorgeous copperplate, with each repetition a growing smile of assurance and pride registering on his cheeks: *My name is Oswald Eugene Mosilyo, secretary-treasurer of the Lesotho Western Engineering Company Limited's Ladies' Netball Team (Undefeated Middle Regional B-Grade Champions 1993–1996, Runners-up 1997–1999).* It was easy to imagine the neatness of the team ledgers back in Lesotho, and that all the balls, whistles and uniforms were accounted for.

But even Oswald couldn't control the intrusive general prison chaos that made her task difficult, that regularly made her frown and grimace and hold her stomach as if in chronic pain. Her class was held in the frenzied two hours between two p.m. and four p.m. known as 'free time', when B-wing prisoners were allowed out of their cells to watch videos on a communal television, line up to use the phone, buy soap and toothpaste and Mars bars, and attend education classes. So Angeline's class competed with violent movie car chases and explosions, a table-tennis competition and a beginners' drum class next door. Without apology, warders constantly poked their heads in to snatch out some prisoner or other. Youths changed their minds and came and went into the education cell with no idea what 'creative writing' was, or even 'English'. One boy peered in to ask the same question every week: 'Miss, will you braid my hair *creative* like yours?'

'Sorry, Winston,' she said. 'I'm not a hairdresser. But I'll give you a book to read.'

'Oh, man. You're the *creative* teacher. I need a creative style. Maybe next week.'

'Don't come back, son,' growled Oswald.

Pablo Dyson was one student who listened intently to Angeline's quiet instructions and obeyed them as best he could, even if it meant taking his eyes off her for minutes at a time. Already he lived for those two hours on Thursday afternoons. Just to surreptitiously inhale her, and hear her lilting voice – so roundly formed and sweet and earthy – and fantasise about the texture of her lips, and more. He could have eaten her sweet, decent words as they ventured out into the air.

He attempted every writing exercise she suggested. Point-of-view. Plot. Description. Tense. Characters. He was perfectly happy to oblige, to write in the first person or in the present tense if she wanted him to. He'd gladly try her tricky stream-of-consciousness paragraphs, like writing without using adjectives or the letter E. To please her was his aim; to claim the smallest smile or encouraging spark from Angeline Shehabe was the main event of his week. Along the way, he didn't mind setting down certain parts of his life. It helped fill in the time; there couldn't be much longer to wait until he was out of here. If it helped him understand what had gone wrong and how he could have come to this, he guessed that was a bonus.

※

At night the prison reminded Dyson of an aquarium, the old one at the harbour wharf with the tin shark on the roof. The same subterranean atmosphere, public-toilet marine smell, damp walls, humid air and over-bright artificial light. A dank place where the smaller, more pallid inhabitants flicked aside as the sharks cruised through. And he felt like a foolish child, a dozy kid visiting on a school excursion who'd been inadvertently locked in after closing time.

Foolish? He'd been heading for Sennen Cove in Cornwall and Freshwater West in Wales and a highly rated right-hand reef break at Thurso East in Scotland, bare expenses and a low-budget, extra-long-haul Garuda flight provided by a weekend travel supplement that liked his novel idea of a European surf-spot appraisal. He'd already surveyed Portugal and France. Variable waves, wild girls. At Heathrow,

THE AQUARIUM AT NIGHT

Customs found four ecstasy tablets in one of his board bags. Four old sandy, linty, waxy tabs jammed in the side pocket with the spare leg-rope and board wax.

He had no memory of them. Presumably he'd been given them while still heavily jet-lagged. There was a dim recollection of a lively beach club in Guéthary on the Basque coast, and a tall giggly girl with spiky red hair. While the Home Office considered whether he was guilty of drug smuggling, with its severe custodial sentence, or merely illegal possession – a far more lenient penalty – he was charged with both offences and remanded without bail. A passport stamped with visas for Indonesia, Peru, Thailand and Brazil didn't help his case. Vigorous protestations that he was a professional surfer, not a drug smuggler – that trying to smuggle four ecstasy tablets into Britain made no sense; coals to Newcastle, like taking a bloody teaspoonful of coal to Newcastle! – cut no ice with the authorities.

'Why would I bother, why take the risk, when I can buy them in any club in London?' he told the investigators. 'Can you now, mate?' they said, as their searching Stanley knives enthusiastically carved into his two surfboards, sliced into the board bags, his luggage, wetsuits, the soles of his sneakers, the lining of his windbreaker, even *The Da Vinci Code* paperback and toothpaste tube. 'We'll make a note of that.' And after six months inside without bail, his case still hadn't come to court. He was an unconvicted prisoner, in his mind guilty only of stupidity and, at the advanced age of thirty-three, of still being a footloose surf bum. On everything else he was pleading not guilty.

Point-of-view was an interesting exercise. Of course everything depended on your personal standpoint. One side or the other. Guilty or not guilty. Black or white. Right or wrong. His lawyer was optimistic that the smuggling charge would be thrown out as nitpicking. Not enough drugs involved. On the possession count, well, he'd already done six months. When the case finally came up, that would be taken into account. Might be only a week or two left to serve. *When the case came up.* There was a long queue of defended cases ahead of him.

At the aquarium, point-of-view had definitely applied. From the observation deck up above, all the shivering kids *ooh*ing and *aah*ing and pretending to throw one another's caps and bags into the tank, the water below was dark and ominous, seething with invisible denizens, the swirling surface occasionally broken by a stingray's wing tip or dramatic dorsal fin. Peering into the tank at eye level, however, your breath clouding the glass, pressing close to the well-lit fish on the other side, even the circling sharks weren't particularly frightening. The sharks were as lethargic and fat as swimming-pool toys. One of them appeared to have difficulty breathing, the tuna had bite scars, and one stingray's barb was snapped off.

Every afternoon one of the aquarium keepers would don scuba gear and descend into the tank to feed the captive fish. The high point for visitors was him handfeeding the grey nurse sharks. They were surprisingly neat eaters, allowing him to pat them, their teeth daintily missing his fingers by mere centimetres, and at no time did he appear in any danger. Once, when the keeper had climbed out again, young Pablo-to-be had asked him, 'What would happen if you didn't feed them all for a week?'

The man gave him a look. 'What do you reckon, sonny? Use your imagination.'

'Why do the sharks eat the dead fish you feed them and not the live ones swimming past them all day?'

'Habit,' the keeper answered. 'Laziness.'

'How come some of the fish have bite marks on them?'

'Sometimes the sharks forget.'

It seemed difficult to keep ocean fish alive and contented outside of the sea. They didn't look healthy or normal, just existing to be gawked at by people who feared the ocean. Meanwhile, steam misted the glass walls, generators throbbed, pipes sucked up sea water and spat out used water into the harbour, the fish circled incessantly, and gaudy tumours of mould and rust seemed to grow before your eyes.

One Thursday afternoon Oswald Mosilyo was there no longer, apparently transferred to a medium-security prison in Sussex, and shortly afterwards two new students, both white boys, turned up in Angeline Shehabe's creative writing class. The word was they were gang members, either Western Brotherhood or Pastry Crew. As gang members rarely joined either the workforce or the education classes – the gang ethos insisting they shouldn't work for the people who'd locked them up, or become suckhole schoolkid snitches – their presence was unexpected. Angeline looked unsettled by the turn of events. But for now, Dyson couldn't see beyond Oswald's departure being a stroke of luck. It meant he could claim Oswald's seat near Angeline.

Of the four schools of sharks in this particular aquarium – The Muslim Boys, The Asian Peril, The Western Brotherhood and The Pastry Crew – the first three gangs had tacked on some religious, political or racially superior association to enhance their dangerous-outsider status. The Muslim Boys weren't Middle Easterners but black youths whose knowledge of the Koran, say, or even Islam generally, was sketchy to say the least, and whose Caribbean grandmothers probably prayed for them weekly at the Pentecostal Church. The Asian Peril was Pakistani, Indian and Afghan. The two white gangs looked like discarded skinheads or football louts from the '90s, some Western Brotherhood members so heavily tattooed that few white patches remained on their bodies or scalps, and from a distance their skin looked made of blue denim.

With their moist pink hands, floury faces and soulless eyes, the Pastries seemed to Dyson the bleakest and most sinister gang, and the hardest one to fathom. At some stage of their imprisonment they had all worked in the kitchens and they still resembled sly, furtive spit-in-the-soup cooks. Ambiguous in disposition, their gang initiation was said to require both extreme sexual predation and passivity, and because of their rumoured kitchen armoury – more sophisticated than ordinary prison shanks, those run-of-the-mill razor blades set into toothbrush handles – they were otherwise known as the Knives.

One of the new students, his attenuated body and snaggly teeth supporting Dyson's shark comparison, leant over Angeline and presented her with a manila folder. 'Here's my work so far,' he said.

His hands rested on the table just in front of her breasts. Her eyes flicked over the tattooed obscenities on his fingers. She browsed through the folder, frowned and handed it back. 'This is your criminal record, Jason.'

'Twenty-six convictions,' he said proudly. His sharky appearance came from the double row of top teeth that were revealed when he smiled.

'And how old are you?'

'Twenty-three.'

Angeline sighed. She seemed about to double over, as if in pain, but rubbed her stomach and straightened up in her seat. 'Looks like you're going to have a lot to write about,' she said.

While this by-play was going on, the beginners' drum class had started its repetitive *thump-thump-thumpety-crash* next door and the other newcomer, paler and slightly older, with a white-blond buzz-cut and chin fuzz, had seated himself at the end of the table, produced a copy of *The Koran and Science*, opened it at the beginning and begun reading aloud. His delivery was flat and passionless but as he read on, declaring the many deficiencies of Christianity and Western civilisation, his voice rose over the drums until it dominated the room.

Angeline let him read for five or six minutes. Dyson could sense her tension. She was swallowing air and belching quietly, rubbing her stomach and breathing deeply as if to calm herself. 'Thank you,' she finally interrupted the reader. Her voice cracked as she spoke. 'Klaus, is it? Klaus, this is what we do in creative writing class. We do some writing exercises here to get us going. Then at night we try to put them into practice and do our own writing. We draw on our imaginations and experiences and write something ourselves. Then, back in class, we read out what we've written. Our own work. Not something from a book, no matter how marvellous the book is.' Klaus continued reading. The other students were slumped in their seats and their eyes looked wary. 'This isn't a religion class,' Angeline said. 'I respect your views but I think you're in the wrong class.'

Klaus droned on. It was as if she had never spoken, never existed. His accent sounded faintly European and his greenish eyes had the over-bright flair of algal blooms. When Angeline finally stood up from the table he glanced up from his book with a pained expression, as if his scholarship had been interrupted by a menial. 'This is more important than people's immoral teachings. You cannot avoid the truth or prevent the truth. It's all in here,' he said, patting the book. Then he began chanting, staring defiantly into her eyes, his sing-song phrases in jarring counterpoint to the renewed drumbeat next door.

Pablo Dyson was the only prisoner to speak. 'Jesus!' he

said. His instinct was to pat her arm or shoulder but of course this was forbidden. 'Give her a break.'

Klaus was still chanting against the drums when everyone else, apart from shark-toothed Jason and his folder of convictions, began leaving the room. Jason was grinning like a bronze whaler. Dyson stood back to let Angeline through the door ahead of him. For a second he thought he heard Klaus's phrasing change to a hiss as she left.

〜

The prison officers had staged a sudden dawn raid, turning over all the cells in search of a missing spoon and a vegetable peeler, and by mid-afternoon B-wing was still strewn with odd socks, girlie pin-ups, toothbrushes, magazines, squashed ping-pong balls, torn family photographs, smashed keepsakes and ripped-apart pillows. In retaliation for their trashed belongings (the kitchen utensils had not been found), three prisoners had broken a warder's nose and glasses, flooded the bathroom and smashed the table-tennis table, and were now being dealt with.

The tense atmosphere lingered into the afternoon, as if all the early-morning shouting and swearing, the thudding feet and banging of clubs, the lockdown and destruction, had upped the prison's blood-pressure levels. When the cells were eventually opened for 'free time', the Thursday writing students were still edgy, rolling their shoulders and flexing their muscles as they entered the education room.

The drummers were also back in action. Their skills had made little progress and Angeline winced at the noise as she sat down and faced the class. Sitting beside her in Oswald's old seat, Dyson surreptitiously admired her as always, tried to secretly inhale her aroma as usual, and appreciate the buoyant femininity of her presence. Today, however, her arms were crossed around her rigid body, her complexion looked grey, her eyes were bloodshot. At the other end of the table sat Klaus and Jason, leaning back in their chairs, their arms folded.

'Today I want to talk about ignoring the negative voice in your head,' she said. 'This is important for beginning writers. And not only for writers.'

Klaus ostentatiously opened *The Koran and Science*,

extracted a leather bookmark and began to read aloud. Jason was smiling and tapping his blue fingers on the table. The other students turned their gaze on Angeline, their body language still reflecting umbrage at the morning's cell raids, at authority in any guise, even the minimal clout represented by a member of the education staff.

'You're not reading that today, Klaus,' Angeline said.

'Ahmed. My correct name is now Ahmed,' said Klaus. 'Everyone here can witness that this woman is discriminating against my choice of literature, God's only literature. Her presence is not suitable here. An official complaint will be lodged.'

There was silence. Angeline looked dumbstruck, then she blinked several times as if struggling to remember correct protocol and to remind herself that in the economic system of this vast, tight-fisted metropolis she was a black female poet. Klaus/Ahmed began reading again. Jason clapped his tattooed hands. Expressions varying from frowns to smirks played across the faces of the class. Next door a novice drummer began attacking the cymbals.

Pablo Dyson stood then, wearily but determinedly, as

if several difficult personal decisions had been resolved even as a single anxiety – more cohesive but also much weightier – had simultaneously been created. 'One warning only, mate,' he said. 'Get out or I'll shove the book up your arse.'

There was a moment of stunned indecision, then Klaus/Ahmed and Jason scraped back their chairs and left. Five other students exchanged glances around the table and, without speaking, followed them outside, leaving their work and writing materials behind. A discarded pencil rolled off the table on to the floor. Even within the room, Dyson could sense the abrupt change in atmosphere and, beyond that, his own altered status. The muttering and whispering outside was an indication of what lay ahead.

While there was still an hour of 'free time' left, he excused himself from the remainder of Angeline Shehabe's writing class and queued up for the telephone. The call to his lawyer would change his plea to guilty of smuggling. Undoubtedly they'd drop the lesser possession charge. He'd already served six months – an admission of guilt surely couldn't mean more than another few months. And at least he'd know where he stood. There'd be clarity. There would also be Thursday afternoons sitting beside her.

They'd never touch but there would be satisfaction in the watching role, and perhaps there was more to life than physical contact anyway. He would have to be on the alert, impossibly vigilant, but strangely – was this naive of him? – he felt able now to write freely about the sea.

Masculine Shoes

BEFORE LEAVING LOS Angeles to hunt locations for Universal's new tropical island adventure–romance, Tyler Foss searched 'Queensland coast' online and came up with coral reefs, cyclones, crocodiles, ultraviolet radiation, partying high-schoolers, marine stingers and lost skindivers. He also found constant references to paradise on earth. Uncertain terrain, thought Tyler Foss.

As the advance guard, the person at the sharp end of any film project, the veteran Hollywood location scout paid close attention to his image: outlaw-rocker, with a lone-wolf air. He absorbed all the Internet information about white Coral Sea sands, harsh sunlight, rainforest lagoons and salt-lashed boardwalks, gave his clothing the usual careful consideration, and decided, as always, on denim, leather and T-shirts. The only problematical item this time was footwear. Tyler Foss was fifty-five and five-seven, and at all times he wore custom-made cowboy boots.

After his thirty-five years in the business, the cowboy boots, along with the silver ponytail and chin stubble, the chunky Navajo bracelets and the unfiltered Camels, were part of the Foss persona – the Foss legend, he liked to think – set forever in the 1970s. They shouted wise-old-dog-knowingness and keeper-of-celebrity-secrets. And, incidentally, the heels added two inches to his height. He owned two dozen pairs, including boots in ostrich skin (smooth and full-quill varieties), alligator (belly and back), snake (Burmese python and king cobra), lizard, caiman, conga eel, crocodile (Nile and Australian), stingray and kangaroo. But on this assignment much sea-shore reconnoitring over wet sand, cliffs and rocks would be required. Foss's bespoke boots averaged $4500 a pair. On the Massachusetts coast he'd lost his favourite king cobras while scouting *The Perfect Storm* for Warners. The cobra skin had quickly flaked and succumbed to the salty Atlantic fogs. Now for coastal work, regrettably, cowboy boots were out.

An actual cowboy could not have felt more angst at giving them up. Eschewing the boots was a considerable blow to Foss's sense of self. He hadn't worn lace-up shoes, the footwear of the Suits, the Average-Joe citizenry, the office-going nine-to-fivers, since high school. But he was a professional, and intensive research into the best footwear for coastal tramping eventually turned up an alternative: something called the Nature-Grit Sneaker. To Foss the word 'sneaker' had a childish, suburban ring to it, not to mention the off-putting eco-hippie sound of 'Nature-Grit'. But it was made of yak leather, which sounded fairly exotic and hard-hitting, and came in suitably masculine shades: sand-yak, rust-yak, mineral-yak and – presumably for evening wear when traction was needed – black-yak.

Foss got a couple of pairs in sand- and mineral-yak. He was pleased to find they were surprisingly cool and comfortable on the job; moreover that yak skin – perhaps it was the Himalayan high-altitude factor of the beast – really 'breathed' down here at sea level. After a long day's tramping through rainforest humidity or sand-dune heat, even without socks, they smelled less than regular sneakers. And, as he'd discovered on the Gold Coast, if you wished to undress quickly, especially after an evening's drinking, they required far less time and effort than boots. Cowboy-boot removal, Foss had to admit, could cost a man valuable impetus and energy these days, with sometimes depressing results. As well, the Nature-Grits were about $4000 cheaper than, say, his alligator bellies or conga eels. He could almost forgive them for the missing two inches.

For the whole late-autumn month of May – according to his research a dry, benign, season-turning month in Australia, when anything cyclonic, venomous or man-eating should be absent or dormant – Foss roamed the north-eastern seaboard in his yak-leather sneakers, scouting the required adventurous-cum-romantic 'look' for the film, which was set on an unnamed tropical island in an unnamed ocean. And neither daytime saturation by sudden tidal surges nor nighttime bar spillages and nightclub and casino scuffing could mar his Nature-Grits. Surf, salt, rocks and reefs, beer and bourbon drips, Camel ash: the yak leather resisted them all.

Despite the effortless professionalism of his new shoes, however, even after three weeks' extensive searching, no coastal location seemed quite adventurously romantic enough *in an original Tyler Foss way* to recommend to the producers. He was becoming worried.

At an anxious ebb, Foss lugged his cameras and battered leather duffle bag (the sort that brought pirates or World War II air aces to mind) aboard a tourist ferry to an offshore island famous for its translucent sands. And as the boat slowly chugged along the scenic eastern shore, allowing the passengers their holiday snaps of migrating humpback whales, his anxiety began to fall away. How was it possible for a lagoon to be so clear, for a beach to be even whiter than the coral shores he'd just left? This sand was like crushed pearls. What excited him as the boat drew closer, however, was the dramatic potential of the ornately rooted pandanus palms, lawyer vines and shadowy eucalypts poised on the edge of those pale sand-hills. The stark vegetation provided a sinister backdrop to the serenity of the shore. Winter storm tides had eaten into the dunes, and undermined trees lay toppled on the beach all along the high-water mark. Their exposed roots and claw-like branches now gestured at the sea and grabbed at the sky.

Lustrous sands, accessible jungle, crystal seas and menacing trees; Foss couldn't snap shots quick enough. He had a good feeling about this place: it should more than satisfy the director's and production designer's creative visions. The producer, too: the island was conveniently situated only thirty minutes from the mainland. Curiously, it did seem to be inhabited by many lean and tawny stray dogs, but as Foss and the other ferry passengers disembarked, the dogs skulked into the shadows of the wharf pylons and vanished into the rainforest. Easy enough for the animal wrangler to keep them out of frame, mused Foss absently, checking into his hotel.

His immediate task that first afternoon was to take some offshore photographs of the island. Leaving the sand-yak sneakers on the beach, he rolled up his jeans and waded out into the shallows. For perhaps an hour, until the tide began to turn, he snapped away determinedly, capturing the main beach from many vantage points before wading back to shore. Strangely, he couldn't find his sneakers anywhere. They were gone. Stolen.

For a few minutes, Tyler Foss stamped the sand in fury and frustration. There was no one else around now. What sneaky son of a bitch would steal a man's shoes from the beach? Because he prided himself on travelling light, he'd packed only one other pair of shoes, the mineral-yaks. But eventually, taking deep breaths, he told himself life would go on. He'd suffered worse tribulations than bare feet and stolen footwear – pneumonia, for example, while scouting sites for *Cold Mountain* in Romania (Romania had to pass for Virginia and North Carolina). Not to mention the king-cobra boot disintegration in Massachusetts. As dusk began to fall, his temper finally settling, he padded back to the hotel with his first island location shots.

〰️

Showered and re-shod an hour later, his sanguinity returned, he sauntered out into the hotel gardens in order to have his customary end-of-the-working-day Camel and Jim Beam, to plan the next day's schedule, and to see what the night might bring. *Seeing what the night might bring* was Tyler Foss's favourite part of the day. Mostly the night brought nothing but a hangover, of course, but he was an evening-optimist by nature, perhaps unusual in someone thrice divorced. Ever since he was sixteen, a short, pimpled boy showering before a movie date at the neighbourhood Rialto, this magic time of day had filled him with hopeful anticipation.

Anything could happen, especially in hotels; especially in hotels in foreign parts. As he well knew, when people were overseas, or on ships or islands, they did things they would not do at home. It was something to do with the sudden separation by water, the partition from their ordinary lives. And watching the last pink streaks of sunset fading between the coconut palms, and the deft fingers of the cocktail waitress adjusting a frangipani in her hair, he felt the old anticipative frisson.

As he sipped his drink, Foss became aware of some activity involving ladders and wires at the far end of the hotel gardens. A local film crew was bustling about and setting up under the palms. What was this? Already he felt a territorial imperative: this was *his* film location. He collared a passing gaffer and discovered they were shooting a beer commercial the next day. He tapped the loose shreds from a Camel, lit up, and through a spurt of smoke magnanimously informed the gaffer, 'I'm in the business myself.'

When the crew finished setting up, he invited them to join him for drinks. He was loudly convivial, as if he and they really were in the same industry, as if these Aussie TV-commercial makers and Universal Studios were even on the same planet. But they seemed amiable company, quite awed by him, in fact, and as far as he was concerned any film crew in the world held more possibility of night-time action than a garden of tourists.

Meanwhile the production assistants kept consulting clipboards and frowning at their watches, on the lookout for the commercial's director, producer and art director, and eventually there was a dramatic clattering in the darkening southern sky and from the direction of the Gold Coast came a helicopter. It hovered for a moment before landing by the swimming pool, discharging the people Foss's drinking companions were expecting, plus an attractive woman in a short banana-coloured skirt that accentuated her legs.

'That'll be her,' remarked one of the production assistants, with respect in her voice. 'That's the octopus stylist.' And it was. The octopus stylist had multihued bird's-nesty hair, a chirpy manner and a confident pointy chin reminiscent of the actress Reese Witherspoon. Tyler Foss was an old hand but he couldn't recall ever meeting an octopus stylist before, or even considering the possibility of their existence. From the moment of their meeting, however, when she generously joined the crew for drinks and ordered a mango daiquiri, he imagined that for the rest of his life whenever the subject of octopus styling came up, he would think of her.

~~~

Her name was Mia McKenzie. On the crew sheet she was listed as 'cuisine art director' but her bailiwick was seafood and her forte was cephalopods. Octopus, squid, cuttlefish. Her job was styling them to look attractive on camera. Apparently, she was in great demand for television, magazines and coffee-table food books. Her professional brief this time was to turn a smorgasbord table of molluscs and crustaceans into an artistic display to sell more beer.

This TV commercial was intended to change the image

of beer drinkers as sweaty, blue-collar pie-eating men with bulldozers and cattle dogs. (Those people drank lots of beer already.) The nation's middle-class women needed to be shown what a sophisticated and natural image a glass of beer could give them. Hence the presence of six lean-waisted extras in a tropical island party setting, all wearing white, raffishly crumpled natural fibres while enjoying glasses of beer in the vicinity of tastefully designed fresh seafood. Hence Mia McKenzie's octopus styling. It had nothing to do with eating. It would be an exhibition, however fleeting its eventual moment on screen, to illustrate the sophisticated yet natural world of today's beer drinker.

All this Tyler Foss gathered as he competed with the crew for her attentions. For once his own range of impressive and scandalous Hollywood anecdotes was forgotten; he was tongue-tied by her rainbow hair, endless legs and vivacious manner. 'Lobsters are a cinch,' she was declaring. 'A spray of glycerine and they look fabulous. And crabs, too, once you've oiled them. Prawns, whole fish, oysters – any smelly old fish shop can style them. They're all a cliché.' She was waving her arms for emphasis. Chopping the air. 'The shiny red lobster, symbolising passionate life, although actually boiled to death. The dramatic aggression of crab claws. The pink excess of a mound of prawns – just an invitation to gluttony. The oyster's sexual associations. Give me a break. Old, old hat. It's the octopus that stretches your imagination.'

'I can see how it would,' he said. 'All those legs. Or are they arms?' Oddly adolescent and awkward in her company, he gave a snorting laugh which accidentally turned into a tobacco cough.

Her look was suddenly wary. 'Yes, there are those to consider,' she said.

'What about squid?' he asked. He couldn't believe he was labouring this conversation. 'There's no way a squid looks edible,' he stumbled on, self-consciously. 'Very ugly suckers.' His accent, thickened by bourbon and cigarettes, rumbled in the night air. 'I don't think I could style a squid,' he heard himself say. 'I guess I'd be more of a beef stylist.'

Mia McKenzie was staring at him now, squinting slightly, as if she normally wore glasses and wanted to really register his presence. The grey ponytail with its tinge of nicotine yellow, the elderly white stubble, the chunky turquoise and silver Navajo bracelets, the ageing-rocker garb. 'Yes, I've met a few homely squids,' she said, and turned her attention to the young assistant director on her other side.

Last drinks were called then. 'Nightcaps in my room!' announced Tyler Foss, ever optimistic.

'We're shooting first thing,' someone said firmly, and within a few seconds the film crew had swept up the octopus stylist in their tide and surged out of the gardens. Alone, Foss stubbed out his final cigarette, sighed, stretched out his feet in their mineral-yak Nature-Grits. So much for comfort; without his cowboy boots he'd lost height and panache. He'd mislaid his humour and banter, and his successful way with women in foreign places. Wearily, he got up from the table. Apart from some night creatures rustling in the bougainvillea, the distant throb of surf and the sudden hum of the pool filter, the hotel garden was silent.

≈≈

Rising at dawn as always, Tyler Foss washed down some aspirin with orange juice and set out along the western shoreline to take more reconnaissance shots. The tide was out, a light fog blurred the horizon and his eyes watered in the sudden sharp sea air. A pale flurry of ghost crabs parted at his approaching steps, panicked back and forth, scattered into three groups, then re-formed and continued to bustle alongside him. For perhaps twenty minutes he strolled along the shore, occasionally snapping photographs, before he reached the eroded dunes and collapsed trees. This was what he was looking for. This tortured beachscape would seal the deal. Already he could visualise the stark scenes on-screen. And then he sensed he was being followed.

He turned quickly. There was nothing there. Only the dead fallen trees and twisted roots and the sheer sand-cliffs rising up behind them. The morning's only sound was the soft, wheezing rattle of the restless ghost crabs, like an asthmatic's breathing. He resumed walking. Again there was the feeling of being followed. Again he turned sharply. Nothing. He felt foolish and childish, like he was playing Grandmother's Footsteps or What's the Time, Mr Wolf?, reliving the suspense of those childhood games and feeling his heart beating faster. But this time he noticed prints in the damp sand, eerily close behind his own. Paw prints.

Tyler Foss stood completely still and eventually a thin, ochre-coloured dog emerged from a tangle of tree roots. Then an identical second dog. The dogs, both males, started silently circling him. He waved his arms and growled at them with all the throaty timbre of 200 000 Camels. The dogs kept circling, as if judging their opportunities. Foss wished he had one of his shotguns with him. The Browning 525. He recalled something from an African location foray and took off his T-shirt and stretched it above his head to make himself look bigger and more threatening. Apparently, it worked with leopards, animals unfamiliar with shirts, but the dogs didn't appear the least threatened. Soon another dog, a bitch, joined them. Foss threw stones and driftwood at them but the dogs took no notice, allowing his stones to bounce off their ribs as they slunk towards him on their bellies.

Then a flash of inspiration, born of survival, struck him. Fumbling with fear, thick-fingered, he undid one of his yak-skin sneakers and threw it to the dogs. Instantly, two of them fell on the shoe, fighting over it. The third dog kept coming for him. Foss tossed it the remaining sneaker – a mineral-yak, his last piece of footwear this side of the Pacific. He left them then, the dogs so busy tearing and devouring their yak meal that they ignored him.

Standing breathlessly at the counter of the general store an hour later, purchasing the only available footwear on the island, a discounted pair of pink rubber thongs, Tyler Foss learnt that he had encountered dingoes.

≈

He began the day's drinking far earlier than usual. Sheltering under a Cinzano umbrella in the hotel gardens, he was shrinking from all contact, human and animal. He was scared to leave the hotel grounds, much less to wander freely around the island. The dangerous dingo problem; the footwear setback: he had much to consider. How could he recommend setting the film here, or indeed in Australia? Four weeks of scouting and nothing to show for it except the career-ending image of a cringing Halle Berry or a pale, shoeless Tom Cruise being bailed up by dingoes.

Under the palms, the beer-commercial shoot was under

way. Foss was on his third bourbon, keeping his distance from the goings-on, when he spotted her bright hair bobbing and glimmering and was drawn by a sad mixture of desire, alcohol and curiosity to the smorgasbord being arranged by Mia McKenzie. That hair of many colours was hard to resist; she was the centre of attention as she prepared her display for filming. There was no doubting her status. Compared to her artistic endeavours with octopuses, squid and cuttlefish, the ministrations of the other food designers seemed insignificant, merely cheap craft. Even the usually superior ice carvers looked faintly ashamed of their melting dolphins.

Passing women – tourists and crew members alike – were shaking their heads in admiration as they spied the octopus stylist's presentation. Men, of course, hung in besotted fashion around her busy limbs and parrot hair. Wielding cans of canola oil, glycerine and hairspray, her fingers a blur of motion, dabbing here and there with pastry brushes, spraying and anointing and smearing, rearranging errant tentacles and erecting complex cephalopodic structures with hidden toothpicks, she was sculptor, engineer, architect and painter.

'Your feet!' she yelled suddenly. 'Love your feet!'

She'd spotted him. Tyler Foss flinched, waved an embarrassed hand, and on his $3.50 ladies' thongs began to flip-flop back to his sheltering umbrella.

'See you at the wrap party tonight!' she called out.

So of course he turned up at the party. And inevitably the octopus stylist was being swamped with male attention. All evening she was trailed by some infatuated actor, electrician or assistant producer. But she handled every overture as deftly as she'd managed the day's suckers and tentacles. At two a.m. her laughter still trilled from the hot tub. Beside her in the warm bubbles reclined Tyler Foss. Mia McKenzie put down her daiquiri, laid a hand on his arm, and eased closer. Tonight the distant party buzz and the surge and gush of the hot tub drowned out the pulsing of the surf. The gardens were quiet. Even the four dingoes bolting down the seafood display under the palms made no sound.

'You make me laugh,' she was saying to him. 'The pink thongs, fracturing your image, turning it on its head. I love that.' One thing Tyler Foss was good at was reading the signs. So he went with the flow of the evening and kept the outlaw-rocker dude more or less under control.

Next morning the helicopter came for her ridiculously early. But, as she said to him, there was no time to waste. There was calamari to be arranged in Noosa.

The Cartoonist

OF COURSE ADAM was nervous on his first day at the new school, a north-coast high school that seemed to be populated entirely by surfers and swimsuit models. Everyone had the blond confidence of teenagers from TV soaps, whereas at thirteen he was a thin, ginger boy with indoor-looking skin and a tendency to do an odd thing with his mouth when he was anxious or focusing on something.

His mother called it 'Adam's concentrating face'. His tongue stretched unbidden over his top teeth and settled there under his lip, the underside displaying thick purple veins, until the moment of anxiety or absorption passed, or until someone laughed at him. He did the mouth thing when he was on the computer, when he sharpened a pencil, or peeled an orange, or tried to catch a ball. Then if he missed the ball (a sixty/forty chance) he did it out of shame and embarrassment. When he made the concentrating face most intensely, however, was while he was drawing.

He had a talent. Whenever he was bored or nervous, or just filling in time, he drew cartoons. Mostly cartoons of people, humorous or grotesque caricatures, although he'd drawn a serious pencil portrait of his mother sitting on the sofa when they first arrived up here – when they were sort of bonding, just the two of them together now – which she'd stuck on the fridge, and one of his father, from memory and an old photograph, which he kept in his room. Sometimes, in the privacy of his bedroom, he was also compelled to do sexy drawings, which he immediately tore into shreds and flushed down the toilet. Once or twice a scrap of voluptuous breast or mysterious inky black triangle had bobbed to the surface to mortify and panic him hours later.

Less guiltily, perhaps because his own nose had suddenly grown into a bit of a honker, pink and often pimpled, and the rest of him showed no signs of catching up, he specialised in noses. If he could get noses right, he reasoned, the rest of professional-grade cartooning would follow. So he slavishly copied the nose styles of popular cartoonists and comic-strip artists, noses in direct left and right profile, half profile and front-on. (*The Phantom*'s nose was his favourite model, a Roman nose combining strength and nobility.) He'd start with the nose and then flesh out the particular face and body around it. He drew nose-based people on the covers and in the margins of his schoolbooks, on his desk, everywhere. As he drew them, his own face – the concentrating face – would unconsciously turn itself into a sort of cartoon, too. When he did the mouth thing it stretched his nose even further down his face and bared his nostrils to the world.

Naturally he'd been made aware of the concentrating face; kids had been laughing at it ever since kindergarten, calling him 'Monster Face' back then. Unfortunately, focusing on *not* doing the mouth thing brought on a compulsion to do it. In a new place 900 kilometres from his old inner-city haunts, at a new school, and living now just with his mother, he was concentrating especially hard on not making the concentrating face. It was preying on his mind.

He stood out anyway because he was the only boy wearing the school uniform. To get the starchy newness out of it, he'd made his mother wash it, but he hadn't expected everyone else to be dressed in scruffy surfwear. And there was his hair problem. Old people sometimes ruffled his hair nostalgically and called him Bluey. On the bus coming north an indignant old codger had announced to all and sundry, yelling down the aisle as if Adam weren't there, 'You know why you don't see much red hair these days? It's been bred right out of Australians. Blame all the wogs with their black hair.' Then he'd winked at Adam, handed him a dollar and said, 'There you go, Blue, buy yourself an ice cream.' He didn't want an old man's dollar; anyway what sort of ice cream could you get for a dollar these days? He was feeling strange in any case because of the way they'd left so abruptly, his mother believing her wedding anniversary an appropriate date to flee north to 'find' herself. The old man on the bus didn't have any hair at all, red or otherwise. Adam wished red hair had indeed been bred out of his family, and the freckles and pink nose that went with it.

In this new classroom he was too nervous to attempt

any public drawing just yet. However, by fiddling with his hair – dragging it over his ears in hopeful imitation of the other boys' salty and stringy surfer hairstyles – and staring out the window at the ibises stalking sandwich crusts in the playground, he was confident he'd managed to avoid doing the concentrating face during morning classes: double maths and geography. It was probably a good sign that by lunchtime no one had spoken to him or paid him any attention. They were very deadpan kids up here.

At the canteen he queued for a meat pie. The jostling could almost have been accidental. In any school, bigger boys shoved and bustled you and trod on your feet; he was used to it. He bought a pie and eventually found a seat by the toilets next to a girl with smeary glasses and a hearing aid. Unfortunately the pie was one of those deceptive ones: coolish crust outside and molten gravy inside – and, for all he knew, molten buffalo eyelids, camel tendons and pig snouts. One bite and his tongue instantly bubbled and his lips blistered. But he supposed it kept him on the right path for the afternoon. His mouth hurt if his tongue even brushed his lips, and so prevented him from doing the mouth thing.

No one spoke to him again during the afternoon classes, or on the school bus going home, although from the giggles on the bus and the occasional flicked droplet of some sticky liquid like Coke on the back of his neck he had the feeling that they were speaking *of* him. But at least he'd lasted the first day without incident or major embarrassment. Things were sort of neutral. Neutral was the best that could be expected. Neutral even counted as a success. So did remembering the correct bus stop for the cottage his mother had rented up here.

From the bus stop it was a long winding walk uphill, cow paddocks on both sides of the road, creatures rustling in the bushes, the occasional lonely-looking horse staring at him over a fence, and every so often a brush turkey racing back and forth in horizontal panic. Lumps of furry or feathery road-kill, and flattened cane toads as dry as parchment, splattered the road. He was halfway up the hill when a truck sped past him carrying five or six young pigs. They weren't contained or tethered in any way, just loosely loaded in the tray of the truck, and their trotters couldn't grip. When the truck took the bends too fast the squealing pigs all tottered sideways and fell heavily against one side of the tray, then skittered and banged hard against the other. Their squeals sounded all the way up the hill, and even after the truck had disappeared.

What sort of sadist was that truck driver? Adam wondered. Now he felt guilty having had the pie for lunch, and as he tramped up the hill he fantasised briefly about becoming a vegetarian vigilante who dealt violently with cruel stock transporters.

He was still in a daze about the pigs and vegetarianism when he arrived home, so for a moment he didn't notice the car parked outside the cottage, camouflaged by the overgrown bougainvillea and lantana thicket. Surprisingly, the cottage's front door was locked. The back door was locked, too, but there were people inside because he could hear panting and grunting.

When he pushed against the door, the bolt rattled and the noises stopped abruptly. Adam stood by the back door for several minutes. He didn't knock. It was now silent inside the cottage and he had the feeling that not only he but all the people on earth, from Tibet to Brazil, were holding their breath. Eventually he inhaled one very deep breath himself, let it out, then walked to the farthest back edge of the property, deliberately out of earshot in the long grass, not caring about snakes or ticks, and sat on the raised roots of a Moreton Bay fig, facing away from the cottage into the wind. The tree itself was long gone – struck by lightning, blown over or chopped down – but its buttress remained.

He knew it was too far away but Adam stared hard into the southern horizon in the direction of the city, trying to discern it through the clouds and the sea mist and the silhouettes of distant trees. The present and the future were a mirage too hazy and skewed to contemplate, so he thought of the simple, clear years past, and people and things that were suddenly absent. He thought of his father down in the city doing mundane fatherly things: replacing light globes, checking the car radiator, watching football on TV, exiting the bathroom with the morning paper, and his, Adam's, favourite memory of him, scraping sodden leaves out of the roof gutters one Saturday afternoon years ago, and laughing as leaf mulch dropped on his head and settled there like a muddy clown's wig. When they'd left him he was crying, a unique and terrible sight, like someone in a film, sitting alone on the veranda behind the Beefmaster barbecue they'd given him two Father's Days ago.

Then Adam heard the toilet flush, and an unfamiliar cough, and the weight of his new school backpack suddenly registered. It was still on his shoulders. He dumped the bag on the ground and took out one of his new exercise books and a black pen. Furiously, gripping the pages tight against the southerly breeze, he began to draw.

To warm up, he drew noses first, then drew himself, his own big-nosed face in savage free-flowing close-up. Then he found a fresh page and began to draw a naked couple having sex – crude, exaggerated, public-toilet-wall sex. What he'd do was slide this drawing under the cottage door. As he focused on the cartoon, his concentration forced his tongue and teeth and lips so hard together that in his grimace he tasted blood.

Prometheus and Greg

IN THE BAR of the Reef Hotel I saw an old, weather-beaten man drinking a schooner of beer by himself, sipping it slowly as if to make it last, and gazing out through the pandanus trees towards the ocean. His face, although deeply lined and morose, rang a bell from my childhood. It took me a long while to place him (the inapt pearl ear stud threw me off) and by the time I'd remembered a cheerier version of him, he'd finished his beer and shuffled off into the wind. Alf Holland. Of Alf Holland Motors.

In my youth, Alf Holland was a big wheel in this town, a leading motor-dealer at a time when the motor car attracted more reverence than it does nowadays; when to present new Holden cars to the Australian public, especially if you featured prominently in your own television commercials with the release of each year's model, was as estimable a social position as being a chef, racehorse trainer or hairdresser is today.

In the heyday of Alf Holland Motors he was ubiquitous: president of the local Chamber of Commerce and a member of every sporting club, charity and Catholic Church committee in town. He wore bow ties, proper ones, which in itself was almost enough to make him a public figure back then, and he spoke in a lazy semi-American drawl, with constant references to General Motors, that mythical country whose empire he served so diligently.

At his most celebrated stage he made the front page of the local paper, the *Northern Sun*, by brazenly swapping our sunny coastal shores one Christmas for the ski slopes of Aspen, Colorado. Another time he made the paper by learning to sail ocean racers and then entering the Sydney to Hobart yacht race. But mostly Alf Holland was pictured shaking hands with a nun or a boy scout or a lifesaver or someone in a wheelchair while handing over an outsized cardboard cheque for thousands of well-publicised dollars. Those were the halcyon days for the Holland family.

I went to St. Joseph's with his sons, Alan and Greg. It would be hard to imagine two more different personalities or physical types than those brothers. Greg, the elder by two years, was a handsome muscular boy, a star athlete, football captain and, to any observer of the family, his father's favourite. Alan was my age, short, chubby and scholarly, usually top of our class, and a mother's boy barely tolerated by his older brother. Alan was late to mature, whatever that condition is called, and with his smooth pink cheeks and unbroken voice he was still being called on to play female roles in our school plays at the age of sixteen.

Fortunately for Alan, bullies tempered their worst attacks on account of Greg being his older brother – not that retribution would necessarily have followed; Greg seemed to ignore his existence. Of course Alan was regularly taunted. But somehow, through brains and guile, he prevailed at this tough, sporty, all-boys school. I remember we other sixteen-year-olds sniggering at his pure high voice in *Joseph and the Amazing Technicolor Dreamcoat*, just as I recall him bringing notes from his mother about 'glandular problems' to excuse him from cadet camps and sport – and, presumably, from the humiliation of the showers and the change rooms.

Greg's sporting ability heralded a big future. As they always do, the football-crazy Christian Brothers advocated a stellar league career, but track-and-field and cricket fame were also possibilities. It was just a matter of him deciding which sport to favour with his attention. Unfortunately, as well as strength, speed and superlative hand-eye coordination, Greg had a sulky disposition, little conscience, a short attention span, and a late-night girl habit on the eve of exams and big sporting events. Maybe the temperament and the athletic ability went hand in hand. But even from my vantage point two classes below (and most younger boys hero-worshipped him), his high opinion of himself, the impression he gave that he'd already made it to the top, seemed premature.

On leaving school, bankrolled by Alf, he travelled overseas for a year to surf and ski at various famous locales. Once back home again, however, while he continued to seduce the district's best-looking girls as if he were checking off a list, he had trouble settling into steady employment. University was out of the question. Similarly, as his night-life blossomed he showed little inclination to train hard enough for serious sporting success. Like many men before him, he seemed destined to leave his athletic brilliance behind on the school playing field. Much of the town, however, still regarded him as a glamorous figure. Boys respected him for his natural ability, his way with women, his knockabout nature. And while condemning the stupidity of any girl who got involved with him, most young women who gossiped about Greg Holland's dreadful exploits did so with a trace of wistful envy.

Increasingly, though, as he passed through his twenties and entered his thirties, he still gave everyone the impression that the world owed him a living and that the world wasn't accepting this proposition with sufficient speed and enthusiasm. It wasn't as if he hadn't already had an armchair ride. Through his father's influence, many jobs were offered. Over the years Greg dabbled in luxury-boat sales, real-estate development and motel management. He was lucky to live in a benign coastal town where all that really mattered was that you grew up there. And if your parents and grandparents had, too – well, as long as you were easygoing and turned up at the office, you could make money and be successful. And his family had been settled there for three generations.

But Greg stretched the usual tolerance of the town business network to breaking point. He was energetically shiftless. He'd fail to turn up at work for a week at a time, or crash the company car while drink-driving. After lunch he would prowl the office, red-faced and explosive, teasing the juniors and sexually propositioning female colleagues. There was some trouble with company credit cards that was difficult to smooth over, and a notorious late-night incident on top of the billiard table at the Services Club with the club treasurer's seventeen-year-old daughter. After that, Greg's second wife left him and they had to replace the baize.

Everyone had a scandalous Greg Holland anecdote. Then, when he was forty-two, he met a nineteen-year-old swimsuit model named Shauna, a flirtatious package with exquisitely defined features and a taste for expensive weekends on the Gold Coast. Greg cut back on the beer, joined a gym to try to regain his sportsman's physique, and had his chest waxed.

For Shauna he was happy to endure pain; he even had his tattoos altered and embellished. Shauna's name, inscribed within a rainbow arching between his right and left scapula, now brought the earlier panther and great white shark harmoniously together. Greg's shoulder blades told the world he was in love.

Was it inevitable that Greg, drugs and easy money would eventually come together? His own adolescence had preceded the era of dance-party drugs and, anyway, drugs generally had never been to his taste. But Shauna introduced him to certain people. He'd do anything for her, and the money was good. Before long, Greg was doing the Gold Coast run three times a week and was known around the coastal pubs and clubs as GoodHorse Greg.

Interestingly, he was never a user himself. When caught selling three grams of heroin to a Surfers Paradise cop who was dressed, unsurprisingly, as a surfer, he was shocked to discover that being a cleanskin didn't impress the law. Indeed, not being a pathetic junkie who was forced to deal drugs to support his own habit made things worse. The court made an example of GoodHorse Greg, the lowest link in the east coast heroin chain, fined him $5000 and sent him to prison for two years.

Alf paid the fine. Obviously he was shattered by Greg's crime and punishment. For the first time in his life he began to publicly question whether he had failed in his paternal role. With some reservations (he was a widower now, retired and seventy-two years old), Alf agreed to Greg's plea to look after Shauna. Before long, to the astonishment of his old and equally hirsute cronies at the surf club, Alf experienced his first chest, back and shoulder waxing, started attending the gym every morning, and began singing the praises of Viagra. He also sported a pearl stud in his left earlobe, the earlobe that announced that, yes, Alf Holland was a heterosexual stud himself, and in love. Expensively so.

That had the whole town talking, too. As did the melange of misgivings that Alf faced on his son's release on parole eighteen months later. In the interim, Alf's life had dramatically changed. The Shauna question loomed uncomfortably ahead. What to say to Greg? Indeed, what to say to Shauna? What to expect? Shauna settled the question herself by announcing she 'needed time to think'. To help clarify her thoughts she moved in with Hans, a twenty-four-year-old professional waterskier at Sea World. 'It's OK,' she mollified her elderly mentor. 'Hans is gay.'

Father and son were uneasily reunited. To each, the other had changed in discomfiting ways, but Alf organised a big welcome-home party for his son aboard his cruiser on the Brunswick River. Later, the party would be painstakingly discussed. Witnesses' reports had to be gathered for the coroner. People said Shauna's laughter seemed brittle, there were confusing undercurrents on deck, raised voices below deck, and various combinations of guests exchanging meaningful or questioning glances. But the champagne flowed and an expensive caterer from Byron Bay served delicacies as far removed from prison food as possible. (No, definitely no drugs. Of course no drugs were on offer or evident on board. This was Alf Holland's party. Formerly of Alf Holland Motors.) At dusk, Alf anchored below the traffic bridge so if anyone wished they could cool off.

The suggestion was generally unappealing. The river was running red and frothy after weeks of rain on the volcanic soils of the ranges. For the possibility of reckless physical display, however, all heads still turned towards Greg Holland – and he didn't disappoint them. Eighteen months on a prison diet had thinned him down. He seemed keen to show everyone, especially Shauna, that he was the lithe sporting hero once more – and that he was back.

Greg climbed on to the roof of the wheelhouse, the highest point of the boat, and, to general cheers, dived into the loamy water. With the tide's assistance, he swam to the sandbank in the middle of the river and, without pausing for a breather, turned around. But now the currents were against him. The harder he swam, the further away the boat seemed. The murky currents swirled and tugged, and the unaccustomed champagne and his lack of stamina began to tell. He swallowed a mouthful of dirty water and began coughing. As the tide was pulling him towards the river mouth and the open sea, there was music playing on board and Shauna was on deck in her bikini, dancing and laughing, and he threshed even harder. It was then that GoodHorse Greg's heart gave out.

PROMETHEUS AND GREG

All this was the talk of the town at the time, five or six years ago. Such was Greg's notoriety and Alf's former community standing that people hardly thought of Alan Holland, or connected him to the Hollands' troubles. As I discovered at a Christmas party down the coast last year, this was partly because he'd long since shunned the family and changed his name.

Knowing few people at this party in another town, I had introduced myself to a group of people about my age. Successful-looking ex-hippies, most of them: Prometheus, Willow Wand, Aquamarina and Colin. Prometheus and Willow Wand looked like a couple, and the way Aquamarina and Colin were stroking each other's arms it appeared they soon might be.

As we exchanged names, Colin remarked to Willow Wand that, sorry, babe, but he still saw her as Sunflower, her former name. By this time I was feeling pretty stodgy in the name department, although Colin was some consolation, his yellow satin pantaloons notwithstanding. During these vaguely uncomfortable introductions, I noticed that Prometheus was very quiet, with an edgy air about him. He'd frowned when we shook hands, as if anticipating some sort of crack about his name, and soon he and Willow Wand had sloped off into the garden.

Aquamarina shrugged. 'Well, we tried,' she said to Colin.

Colin nodded. 'I'm worried about Prometheus, babe.' But he didn't look upset enough to cease fondling her.

Just to make conversation, I inquired, 'Is your friend OK then?' I'd stayed deadpan during the introductions but I couldn't trust myself to say 'Prometheus' without smiling.

'Not really,' Aquamarina answered. 'They won't leave him alone.'

'*They?*' I said.

'It's not important,' said Colin. 'Excuse us.' And he led Aquamarina away towards a large hammock in a jacaranda.

I sneaked a glance at the other couple, now in solemn conversation under a Moreton Bay fig at the edge of the party. Subtract the ponytail and the flowing garments, and Prometheus could have been an earnest Sunshine Coast accountant. Indeed, I realised that his eyes and manner reminded me of someone I used to know. There was the resemblance to Alf, but the put-upon frown was the giveaway. Perhaps I'd even been one of his tormentors years ago. Prometheus was no longer short and pudgy and rosy-cheeked, but tall and gaunt. Alan Holland had taken on quite a responsibility with that name.

An hour later I caught up with a tousled-looking Aquamarina while Colin was fetching drinks. She had shiny eyes, an uneven and rather fetching smile, and a keen interest in native American shamanic beliefs that she was eager to share. She recommended books to me by the authors Wolf Moondance and Sky Starhawk. I wrote the names down. Then I abruptly changed the subject: 'I used to know Prometheus when we were boys at St. Joseph's.' I still had trouble keeping a straight face. 'He's changed,' I added, unnecessarily.

'Everyone changes,' she said, and paused for that to sink in. She gazed around the party as if to check that our conversation wasn't being overheard. 'Some people haven't forgiven him for running off with Willow Wand. Their affair broke up two long-standing relationships. Of course he was Vulcan in those days, and she was still Sunflower. They changed their names for their new life together.'

'Vulcan. More fiery stuff,' I said. I was having trouble imagining Alan, the class brain, straying from a conservative career in the law or medicine, much less little fat boy-soprano Alan having a fiery love life. 'He seems to be sticking close to a theme.'

This was because he was a potter, she explained, with ambitions to be a famous sculptor. When he'd taken up with Willow Wand he'd determined to concentrate on his sculpting. His first major work was a three-metre-high rendering of his namesake from Greek mythology. He had erected it outside their cottage. Striving for mythological authenticity, he'd tried clay at first – Prometheus being the originator of crafts and so on – but he'd ended up fashioning his ultimate Prometheus of bronze, over a skeleton of fibreglass.

The statue was of Prometheus before he ran into the strife with Zeus. The early proud Prometheus, holding the fire he'd stolen to bring to the mortals, not the later Prometheus punished for his hubris, chained to the rock with the eagle pecking his liver for eternity. This Prometheus held aloft the fennel stalk that had brought fire to human civilisation.

According to Aquamarina, 'This was when the trouble started.' The bronze Prometheus had stood outside his sculptor's residence for only a few weeks before they found him one morning dressed in women's underwear, his face garishly made up with lipstick and mascara. Underneath the statue was a sign saying, simply, *Alan*. Aquamarina frowned and said, 'Not many people these days know him by that name.'

Her story continued. Days later his night-time tormentors had begun pelting the bronze Prometheus with fruit snatched from the sculptor's own garden: mangoes, custard apples, bananas. They smeared fruit over his heroic limbs and torso. They rubbed banana paste into his joints, and the acid in the bananas soaked into his skin and after a few days he began to peel. The bronze cracked and started separating from the fibreglass. Prometheus dropped his firebrand. But even mortally wounded, he still gazed proudly over the hilly cattle paddocks and fruit orchards towards Mount Warning.

'What vandals would do that?' I asked her. 'Local kids? Who'd keep going to all that trouble?'

She shrugged. 'They'd made up Prometheus's face again with lipstick and this time the genitals were snapped off. There was another sign underneath: *You Know This is You, Alan*.'

'Jesus!' I said. 'Someone from schooldays.'

'Is that so?' She glared at me now. No spiritual eye-spark any longer, no sweet uneven smile.

'Did he choose to become Prometheus because he was a legendary martyr?' I asked.

She was peering around and beyond me. I could have been a piece of lawn furniture, a palm tree.

'I don't think you understand this,' she said. 'Anyway, Prometheus got free of his chains in the end.'

Aquamarina and I didn't seem to have any more to say to each other. I felt I should approach Prometheus/Alan and reopen our contact. Perhaps I could mention that I'd recently seen his father alone in the pub, and ask him whether he ever saw him. Later, relaxed by a few more drinks, we could talk about our schooldays, maybe even discuss his shift of identity, how interesting it was for him to seek to become someone else, a mythical being, whereas Greg had so badly wanted to stay the same earthbound person forever. And Alf. Alf in his old age had had one last fanciful flight that defied the town's gravity.

I peered around my host's garden and tried to catch a glimpse of the troubled lovers: the mortal Prometheus and

Willow Wand. It was still early evening; dinner hadn't even been served. A four-piece band in Hawaiian shirts was tuning up under the jacaranda. Surely kindred spirits abounded in this mellow scene. But the couple had already left. I turned back to Aquamarina but she had gone, too.

〰️

I asked around town. Apparently Shauna had stayed with Alf long enough to make it financially worthwhile, then vanished. Alf Holland Motors is now a Bunnings hardware store. Alf, in his mid-eighties now, is a familiar lone, leathery figure on the north-coast beaches. He wanders the shoreline, has one beer in the Reef, and leaves. Those brown spots on him look like melanomas to me. His body hair has grown back, a grey pelt like an old wolf, but he still sports the pearl ear stud.

How to Kill a Cane Toad

AFTER THE GUNSHOTS, and the bats' screeching and flapping, they'd lie in bed at night wondering what they'd got themselves into. The blasts, then Janine's agitated fingers tapping on his thigh in an increasingly accusatory way while the bats panicked and stray lead shot pattered on the roof and tinkled down into the gutter: this wasn't how they had imagined country living.

Those lifestyle magazines of hers celebrating a 'tree change' from the city to a simpler existence, where they'd grow organic produce, breathe blossom-scented air, perform rewarding physical tasks in rural clothing while a grazing horse or two added interest to the scenery, somehow never referred to the human element. *Getting back to basics* never mentioned the local inhabitants. Those first weeks, random shotgun explosions had punctuated their daylight hours of vegetable planting, fence mending and house renovation. Now, as a windy spring edged into a humid summer, the shotgun woke them at night as well.

Gunfire is more chilling at night. It came from nearby, but the squally winds and the enveloping orchards and plantations – a dense maze of trees curving and stretching up the echoing hills all the way to the western horizon – made it hard to pin down the source. Down at the general store for the morning milk, bread and newspaper, gritty-eyed from broken sleep, Dan finally asked Cliff Porteous, the proprietor, 'Who shoots guns at night around here?'

Just like Dan's daily presence and purchases – the city broadsheet, the high-grain bread, the low-fat milk – the question appeared to amuse Cliff. 'Oh, old Mango Ken gets shitty with the birds in his trees. Then the fruit bats at night. After a few scotches he decides to scare them away.' Cliff looked on the verge of laughter. 'Don't know when he sleeps.'

He was referring to their nearest neighbour, an orchardist named Ken Riddell. But despite this logical explanation, the day-and-night gunshots, the pellets peppering the tin roof, the shrieking fruit bats and interrupted sleep still unnerved them and soured everything. They woke tired and rattled in the morning and went to bed tired and rattled at night.

This wasn't like a noisy-party problem in the city, where a phone call to the local cops sorted it out; where a constable knocked on the door and told the neighbours to turn it down. An old farmer's livelihood was involved. And 'neighbour' meant something different in the bush. At this early stage they didn't want to come across as arrogant city blow-ins, the sort who moved to the country and then immediately complained about cows and roosters disturbing the peace, and the smell of fertiliser and pesticides.

So their shotgun dilemma not only continued but swelled to include other irritations: Dan's snoring and Janine's increasing abstraction, as well as the area's voracious mosquitoes, speeding motorists, vanishing tradesmen (whenever a good surf was running) and, as the nights warmed and electrical storms blazed and crackled over the Pacific, the sudden appearance and clamour of cane toads.

〰

One mid-December afternoon Ken Riddell stopped his tractor by the dividing fence, introduced himself and welcomed them to the district. So characteristically rustic did he seem in his overalls and tattered straw hat drawstringed under his chin, he could have been a storybook Farmer Giles or Old MacDonald. This was their chance to bring up the nighttime blasts. But how could they start whingeing to him right off the bat when the sociable old gunman was inviting them for drinks that night?

It would have seemed uncivil. And they were grateful to be asked. Apart from smirking Cliff Porteous at the store, Trent Roylance, the estate agent who'd sold them the property, and various elusive, surf-preferring electricians and plumbers, they hadn't met any locals. As they'd watch the sun sink behind the dark corridors of nut plantations and orchards (row upon row of suddenly forbidding trees), sipping oddly unsatisfying gin and tonics, their optimism steadily ebbing with the daylight and the application of mosquito repellent, they'd begun to question, as with so much else, the myth of country hospitality.

But now, with another neighbouring couple, the Eastaughs, also guests this Saturday evening on the veranda of Ken and Elaine Riddell's Federation farmhouse, at least some sort of social life was unfolding. Eagerly anticipating a beer, Dan heard himself break the ice: 'So how do you deal with all these cane toads?' That croaking cacophony, like 100 different telephone dial tones, was beginning to grate as much as the shotgun pellets on the roof.

'Cane toads?' Mango Ken declared, in the over-loud interrogative manner someone might say 'hyenas?' or 'manatees?'.

'Aren't they disgusting?' said Janine, a little too earnestly. 'The way they destroy the wildlife! I hate how they'll eat anything they can fit into their mouths.'

'Toads?' boomed Mango Ken again. As he passed the drinks around, his hands managed four glasses at once. His brown fingers, cracked and swollen enough to burst, looked like pork sausages in the pan. He was eighty-plus, his face the dry yellow of chamois leather, with deep crotchety lines crisscrossing his cheeks and an old-fashioned pink hearing aid like a lump of bubblegum stuck in each ear.

'I Googled them,' Janine went on, raising her voice. (She'd just noticed the hearing aids, too.) 'They're feral, venomous, a scientific import gone wrong. The females produce 35 000 eggs every mating.' Her voice seemed surprisingly shrill. 'How do we fight those numbers?'

A twelve-gauge? Dan almost said.

'The old three wood!' Mango Ken yelled abruptly. His eyes lit up and he stood and teed off, miming a vigorous golf swing. His broad bony shoulders looked as if they still had a bit of toad-belting left in them. He took a swig of his scotch, coughed and cleared his throat. 'If you could be bothered.' He thumped his chest. 'I've got enough on my plate.'

His veranda overlooked forty acres of mangoes, guavas and avocados and, on the higher slopes, ten more acres of Cavendish and ladyfinger bananas. Right now it seemed the Riddells were harvesting about an acre of cane toads as well. Attracted by the swarms of Christmas beetles battering against the louvres, a lumpy carpet of toads was inching towards the house lights.

'No, no, no.' His wife Elaine spoke up. 'Toads don't mind a wallop. It's a waste of time to whack them. By next morning they've recovered and hopped away.'

The old woman put down her scotch and grabbed a plastic shopping bag from somewhere. 'I like to avoid poison spurts!' she shouted, thrusting her hand in the bag. The nearest toad was squatting proprietarily on the back step, calmly licking up Christmas beetles. Elaine stooped down and snatched it up. She must have been hitting eighty herself, but in three deft movements she grabbed the toad in the bag, flipped the bag inside out and tied a knot in it. Like a mouldy windfall mango, lemon-coloured, ovoid and spotty, the toad glared out through the plastic.

'*Voila!*' she said. 'The toad is in the bag.'

'The same way you Paddington people pick up your poodle's poop,' the other male guest, Macca Ken Eastaugh, offered, slyly. He was younger than Ken Riddell by about forty years, but two farmer Kens in the neighbourhood apparently made nicknames necessary. Macca Ken had sixty acres of macadamia trees stretching up the hill behind the Riddells' orchard.

Dan almost pointed out that they'd come from Thornleigh, a far less trendy Sydney suburb than Paddington, and one better suited to a high-school teacher's and librarian's salaries. They'd retired early, taken their superannuation, bought an old farmhouse on acreage, and started – they'd fervently hoped – a serene country life. But he let it go. Country people were forever teasing newcomers. He sipped his beer and said, 'So now you have a cane toad in a bag.'

'Just pop him in the freezer!' roared Elaine, and she opened the fridge and did so. 'And Mr Toad goes quietly bye-byes.'

Dan imagined opening the freezer the next day. In their new life he did the cooking. First thing in the morning he took out the meat to thaw. He thought out loud. 'All those warty frozen toads goggling out from the steak and ice cream.'

'You reckon toads are bad?' said Macca Ken. He was thickset, with an ex-footballer's drum-like torso and a couple of basal cell carcinomas glistening on his nose like half-pearls. 'Try fingers in the fridge.'

'Fish fingers?' said Janine.

'Human,' said Geraldine Eastaugh. 'Human fingers, for God's sake.'

'God's what?' yelled Mango Ken.

Macca Ken rolled his eyes. 'Fingers in the fridge!' He leant back in his chair. 'You tell it, Geraldine.'

'Ken was in the force back in the '80s. Out in the far west even the young coppers had to do a bit of forensics.'

Macca Ken broke in. '*Big* distances to cover in the boondocks. Bodies to be identified. Shotgun homicides. Highway accidents. Imaginative rural suicides. No DNA testing to make it easy back then.' Now he had everyone's attention he paused to take a long sip of beer. 'Hot weather to take into account. If I wanted to finish before dawn, get any sleep at all, I'd snip off the victim's fingers for later ID. Take 'em with me and pop 'em in the freezer at home.'

'I'll say this,' said Geraldine. 'Toad iceblocks are no big deal compared with a freezer full of fingers. Cop them first thing in the morning, they'll wake you up in a hurry. Bitten fingernails, wedding rings, nail polish, the lot.'

For a moment the others fell silent, drinking and gazing out at the patch of toad-filled light on the lawn.

'And I was first trimester at the time with Jade and not keeping anything down.'

'It was easy enough to handle,' said Macca Ken. 'I managed pretty well. Best years of my life in some ways.'

The older Ken had been lost in reverie, nose in his scotch glass, but now he'd had an idea worth mentioning. 'There's always the Dettol method.'

'Dettol?' asked Dan.

'Dettol antiseptic. Give the toads a squirt. Instant death.'

'He dabs it behind his ears, too, before he goes anywhere,' confided his wife. 'Like perfume.'

As if guiltily caught out, Mango Ken turned on her, reddening. 'And I haven't died of paralysis ticks, have I? You get a paralysis tick burrowed in behind your ear and even if you cut the bastard out, your nerves go. You want a face sagging like melted wax, go right ahead.'

'The old bloke's full of good advice,' Macca Ken said, grinning. He raised his voice. 'Tell 'em your hangover cure.'

'Hangovers?' roared the old man. 'Well, you've got your best cure in the world running right round your property. The bloody fence.'

Dan thought of the electrified fence keeping the Riddells' cows out of his new lettuces and tomatoes. He laughed. 'Really.'

'There's enough voltage to really clear the head if you grab the fence with both hands.'

Taking a rise out of the city folks again. 'Oh, sure,' Dan said.

'He's not kidding,' shouted Elaine. 'With a bad hangover, he even wets his hands first.'

'I don't know about you people,' said Janine, 'but I can't stop looking at the fridge and wondering if your toad's frozen yet.'

〜

Although the blasts no longer seemed mysterious or frightening, the nightly hubbub had had its effect. Janine now wore earplugs to bed. They helped block out the gunshots, bats and toads, and also Dan's snoring. The humid summer on top of the noise had pushed him into bad sleep patterns, which developed into a sleep apnoea that made him doze off at inconvenient times in the day and abruptly jerk awake in the middle of the night. When he did pass out, as if to catch up on weeks of lost sleep, he snored loud enough to drown out even the loudest toads.

In his insomniac hours Dan's mind strayed from one anxiety to the next, most of them centred on their precipitous move to the country. His worries centred on Janine, the way her personality and moods were changing. Not only was she blocking herself off from him at night, in the daytime she'd started disappearing for long solitary drives into the hinterland.

More and more he felt cut off. The tree-change adventure had begun with a mutual wish to spend more time together in their middle years. Instead, she was drawing away. She seemed to be seeking a sort of baffling independence. Even her speech patterns, her choice of vocabulary, had become isolating: first person singular. Everything was *I* and *me* and *mine*. When he asked her, 'What happened to *us* and *our*?' she gave him her recently acquired Mona Lisa smile.

'We're all on our individual journeys, Daniel,' she said, smug as a guru.

Daniel? What happened to *Dan*? What bloody journey was this?

Just communing with nature, or *absorbing the environment*, or *exploring the country lanes*, or *getting to know the region*, she'd say enigmatically when she returned home, and briefly mention scenic mountain ridges or pretty waterfalls that she must share with him some time.

Those ridges and cascades and ferny lanes must have been exceptionally picturesque, Dan thought, to distract her for hours afterwards, right up to and including the moment she inserted her earplugs and went to bed.

She was heading to bed increasingly early. Immediately after dinner – no television, no reading, no nightcap, no conversation about the day – she'd yawn and turn in. Earplugged and nightdressed, she'd pass him outside the bathroom, peck his cheek and disappear by 8.30 or 9.00, her heavy sigh coinciding with a similar exhalation from the mattress as she flopped into bed and wound the bedclothes protectively around her.

Of course he asked her if there was another man.

'*Oh, please!*' she said.

What could he do but make a hurt, defiant stand? Faced with her departure from his presence, the brush-off, the shrouded lump on the far side of the bed (not even tropical temperatures dissuaded her from a sheet and blanket), Dan moved into the spare bedroom. Then, rather than face the room's monkish austerity, he began staying up late. He'd finish the bottle of wine he'd opened for dinner as well as the untouched glass he'd poured for her. And as the evening cacophony intruded on his melancholy like a flotilla of approaching motorboats, he'd lurch up from the table, grab the Dettol dispenser and a torch and step outside to kill cane toads.

Dan felt squeamish at first, but he remembered the harm they were doing to the environment. Picking them off with the spray-gun to the sound of intermittent gunshots next door gave toad hunting a mock-military feel. Mango Ken was right. It was a startlingly effective method of execution. One squirt and the enemy instantly imploded, mustering just enough strength to drag itself into the shrubbery, considerately dig its own grave and inter itself.

Pacing around the dew-drenched lawn, half-full of wine,

juggling the spray-gun and torch, strafing the grass, the driveway, the near paddocks, he'd shoot forty, fifty, sixty of the knobbly bastards a night. Like fish in a barrel, really. And why not? The greedy feral trespassers were on the march, south, north and west across the country, gobbling up or poisoning everything – lizards, snakes, rare frogs, birds, insects, fish. The nice, normal Australian wildlife.

No matter how tired, downhearted and confused, no matter how drunk, before facing the spare bedroom each night he had a duty to patrol his territory and kill as many of the invaders as possible.

〰️〰️

It was an overcast March morning with sputtering showers greasing the highway when Dan went for the bread and paper and saw four police cars, three State Emergency Service vehicles and a fire truck pulled up outside Cliff Porteous's store. Radios crackled and personnel were hunched by one of the patrol cars, writing on clipboards, comparing information and sipping takeaway coffee.

Inside the store, the mood was sombre. Local people gathered in small murmuring groups by the magazine racks, eyes glittering with news. Porteous, unsmiling for once, filled Dan in. 'He was on his way here two hours ago as usual,' he said. 'Old Ken Riddell, I'm talking about.' Making a right turn off the Pacific Highway, Mango Ken's car had been broadsided by a tanker carrying milk up to Brisbane. 'Drove right over him. Killed him instantly.'

There was some headshaking about Mango Ken's bad hearing, questions about his eyesight, too; even suggestions that he was too old to be driving. A danger to himself and others. Then again, that section of the highway was a known deathtrap, and it was raining. What had intrigued the police at the crash scene, however, was all the busted shotgun cartridges and loose shot in Mango Ken's car.

≈

That night Dan stayed up even later than usual, killing toads. The earlier rain had softened the soil, moistened the undergrowth and brought toads out in big numbers. When he was prowling about on execution patrol the toads always fell quiet at the approach of his torch, but their sudden stillness tonight didn't explain the wider, deeper silence across the damp lawn and weedy paddocks and surrounding orchards.

As midnight approached, the property was more than merely quiet; there was an eerie absence of noise. A sound vacuum. Of course, he realised, for the first night since they'd moved here, there were no shotgun blasts. And hence no screeching bats, or lead shot clattering on the roof. Without the distraction of noise, the night seemed darker, too, the stars more numerous.

He quickly dispatched twenty-four toads (he always kept a tally). But his pants were drenched and muddy and the night felt uncomfortably humid. Standing alone on the dewy lawn with his spray-gun, the thin beam of his torch seeking the telltale lumps that were distant toads, Dan had a sudden sharp picture of himself as country-dwelling, toad-hunting man. This was the way this dismal creature spent his evenings. Toad Man. The image struck him as too pathetic for words.

And then the air was shattered by a shotgun blast. And

another. A salvo. Pellets tinkled on the roof and pattered on the leaves of the trees and on to his water tank, and fell around him like hail. Another blast sounded, and another. All the fruit bats of the tropics appeared to be whirling and flapping and shrieking over his head. He ran for the shelter of the veranda, deafened and dazed by noise.

Even with earplugs Janine must have been woken by the din because she came out on the veranda, too, and stood on the steps in her nightdress, her arms folded across her breasts, staring into the dark. She was counting the blasts, and continued counting them off aloud. Finally they stopped. 'Twenty-one,' she said.

Self-consciously, he put down the torch and spray-gun. 'What was that all about?' Bats still flapped by them, wheeling and screeching into the sky.

'Looks like Elaine got his guns and gave Ken a twenty-one gun salute,' she said. 'Commemorating him.'

A few stragglers were returning indignantly to the mango orchard. After some territorial squabbling and rustling they settled back in the trees. There was a last protesting squeal and then the bats were silent.

'She probably had a few scotches, and who'd blame her,' he said.

Following the fusillade, the night seemed quieter than ever. Moonlight streaked across the lawn and paddocks. Not quite strangers, more like hesitant recent acquaintances, they stood awkwardly on the veranda, unsure of their next movements. Soon, as if at a given signal, the toads started croaking again, their dissonance quickly swelling to fill the void. Inappropriately, as wrong as a field of outboard motors, an ocean of tractors, they took over the night.

The Rip

THE AFTERNOON AFTER the shark attack, a Saturday in early autumn, a father named John Bingham and his young daughter, Sophie, were strolling south along the Indian Ocean shore. Smoke from an inland bushfire met a humid mist rolling in from the ocean in a haze of muted light across the beach. In the low snapping waves, seashells rattled and chinked like coins. The shells attracted the girl's attention and when she saw a small beached jellyfish amongst them, so perfectly round it could have been drawn with a compass, she gingerly prodded it with a toe.

It was like a translucent saucer from a toy tea set, the tentacles retracted and harmless. 'Will it sting me?' she asked.

'It's OK,' her father said, picking up the jellyfish and placing it in her hand. Just to make sure, Sophie held it at arm's length and the pink of her palm showed through the jellyfish in a diffused way her father found endearing. He hadn't mentioned the shark. Sophie was only five and since the separation she stored up worrying things in her mind.

Although the television crews in their helicopters had come and gone thirty hours before, people still gathered near the point break where the surfer had been pulled from his board. Most of them looked like tourists, their beachwear more seriously casual, their manners louder and edgier than those of the usual whale watchers or deadpan local surfers. A few lone beach-goers stood motionlessly on the headland, as silently expectant as voyeurs. Others hovered noisily on the sand, frowning and chattering, adjusting the brims of their caps and straw hats in the breeze, pointing out to the glassy swells, testing the water temperature, tasting the salt on their lips and inhaling the ozone, as if these actions could help them commit this place and incident to memory and future anecdotes.

How the sightseers wished at this moment for a dorsal fin

to slice through the water and satisfactorily cap their mood — even a humdrum dolphin would be better than nothing. Their imaginations pictured ferocious creatures seething beneath the surface but the only visible sign of marine life was a flock of crested terns rising into the mist and spearing into the slate-coloured sea over and over.

The terns' relentless diving signified a shoal of surface bait-fish, thought Bingham, and the bait-fish meant bigger fish nearby. Many of the people on the beach had come to the same food-chain conclusion. Amid the pointing and murmuring, some of the women shuddered dramatically and unconvincingly, their eyes darting around guiltily in case their enjoyment was too apparent. A couple of teenage boys cackled self-consciously and threw sand and pushed and tripped each other. In several family groups you could make out three generations with similar hair colour and body shapes. The same nervous laughs.

One large matronly-looking woman was even acting the newshound, wading ankle-deep into the ocean, even though fully dressed, while a man on shore, presumably her husband, filmed her describing the attack of the day before. As if she were on the six p.m. news, the woman was delivering a commentary while she gestured out to sea to indicate the tragic point of contact.

A rip was running south near the point; here, there were occasional submerged rocks and muddy corrugations, and once or twice the woman stumbled in the small waves. But urged on by the man with the camcorder she gamely pressed on. A bigger wave broke against her thighs, and then another. Perhaps getting soaked added to the desired intrepid effect because encouraged by the cameraman, and despite her drenched clothes, she adjusted her skirt and continued.

Giggling, Sophie flipped the jellyfish at her father. He threw it back and they made a game of tossing it back and forth. When the jellyfish broke into pieces she fearlessly picked up another and the battle went on until they reached the point and turned back along the beach. But even as they were skylarking, Bingham was thinking how malign the ocean looked, more so than he'd ever seen it. Those gunmetal clouds, now streaked with parrot-coloured flashes of sunset, appeared unnaturally ominous.

Sentiment bubbled to the surface so easily since the

break-up. Suddenly his daughter's existence had never seemed more precarious, their relationship more precious, his love for her more intense. Before the split, the family had swum and played at this beach all the time. On many gentle summer days she'd bobbed in this same parallel tide, teasing him with stabs of fright as her fingers deliberately slipped free of his grasp (his grip, as in a nightmare, still slick from applying her sunscreen) and she allowed herself to be swept up by the rip. Nightmare material again: sweeping along the coast and dragged out to sea, Sophie was a reckless little cork.

Oh no! he'd cry, sharing the delicious mock-fear for maybe five seconds until he'd grab her up, unable to bear it any longer. Now he and Sophie came here only on her visiting weekends. The old familiarity had turned into novelty.

Yesterday's was the fourth beach tragedy this season. The first couple of deaths, simple drownings, hadn't really registered in Bingham's mind but in March a Japanese tourist had been caught in a rip and swept out. He remembered this one because of the unsuccessful two-day helicopter search; a week later, a human femur had washed up in Fraser's Creek, half-an-hour north.

Suddenly his imagination was uncomfortably vivid. The unnatural green and bronze sunset, the perpetual threat of nature and the abruptness of savage chance engulfed the beach in a sombre mood, isolating them from the normality of the coast-road traffic and the bland suburban roofs of the hinterland. The sea had turned sepia. Dusk enhanced the crack of the waves and the aggressive clatter of shells on the sand. Even the hazy air was odd, as if they were peering through smeared glass. The horizon had vanished and it was hard to tell if they were breathing sea mist or bushfire smoke.

Bingham was clutching his daughter's hand when they passed the home movie-makers again. The man with the camcorder was becoming frustrated trying to position the woman correctly. At the same time he was urging more reportorial emotion from her — a louder voice, more expansive gestures — while she was hard-pressed trying to hear his directions and keep her balance in the current. Now she looked self-conscious as her clothes clung revealingly to her bulky body and the rip kept snatching at her legs and shuffling her sideways out of frame.

THE RIP

The cameraman was becoming exasperated. 'Beverley, for Christ's sake, all you have to do is stand still for ten seconds and point to where the shark got him.'

Sophie snatched her father's hand. 'Shark! What shark?'

The woman stumbled again just then, exclaimed an embarrassed little '*Ooh!*' and sat down in the sea. As her skirt billowed around her, she began sailing south in the rip. Both she and her husband looked mystified at this sudden turn of events. The man kept peering at his camera, and then back at her. Meanwhile she continued to sail south. He walked, then trotted, a few steps along the shore after her. Then he seemed to reconsider, slowed again and began shooting this new action.

The woman was picking up pace in the current. Sophie gripped her father's hand. 'Is the lady all right?' The woman was beginning to panic but her husband remained strangely phlegmatic and indecisive. He'd stopped following her along the beach and was still peering through the lens. 'OK, stand up, Beverley!' he called. He sounded irritated. 'You better stand up!'

Bingham kicked off his shoes and moved towards the

water. 'No!' Sophie screamed, and threw herself at his legs. 'Don't go in there!'

'I have to,' he said. 'It's OK, darling, it's not deep.' He prised off her fingers, but she followed him, sobbing, towards the ocean. He had to grab her by the shoulders and sit her down on the sand. 'Don't move!' he said. 'Don't you dare move!' His sudden fierceness was overwhelming and as he left her on the sand she was shrieking.

The two men entered the water together, Bingham heading for the floating woman while the husband followed him, holding the camera above his head to avoid the waves. At that moment the current tumbled the woman to a flat sandbank where, after a couple of attempts, she struggled to her feet. Smoothing down her clothes as best she could, she managed to defy the tide long enough to stagger towards the shore.

'*Yes!*' called her husband, triumphantly, as if he were responsible for this sudden helpful turn in topography and tides. 'Keep coming in this direction.' He was filming her again. As he did so, he recorded his voice saying, 'And here's intrepid Beverley after her big adventure.'

As she got to shore, the woman didn't say anything,

beyond angrily dashing her hair out of her eyes. Then, as she splashed up to him, she struck the camera from his hand into the sea.

As Bingham waded ashore he could just make out his daughter standing stiffly on the beach, a small shadowy stick figure. She was silent now. He tried to draw her to him, but he was soaked and dripping. Sophie pulled away then, and ran up the beach towards the dunes. She sprinted as if from great danger, the sand squeaking sharply under her racing feet.

He reasoned she was running to their car. He wasn't too worried. 'Sophie!' he called after her. 'Stop!' But she kept on, reached the dunes, clambered up the slope and disappeared over the top.

He began running too now, jogging in her footprints, irritated with her, but in his soggy clothes he had no chance of catching up. The dunes were soft, the sand too loose to retain her imprints, especially in the dim light, and surprisingly cold on his feet, cold enough to numb them. The cold spread up his wet limbs to his hips and stiffened his lower back. Eventually he reached the top of the dunes.

Where the sand merged into the loose gravel of the car

park, thick coastal scrub – tea-tree and tuart – grasped the hilltop, and in the trees' crowns birds were squabbling and nesting for the night. Sophie was not at their car. The last few sightseers' cars were starting up, turning on their headlights into the haze, and streaming into the highway traffic.

The roots buttressing the trees reached out like fat fingers. Between the root-fingers some tourist-litterers had carefully inserted their old drink bottles and ice-cream sticks. Bingham spun around, circling the trees, the empty car park, the dank puddles around the change rooms and toilet block, his eyes searching. He heard himself calling her name and repeating into the last smoky streaks of sunset, 'It's all right! Nothing happened!'

The Life Alignment of the Coffee Grower

MY COFFEE DEALER Eric Callahan was contemplating murder. It occurred to me that if he was telling me this, he mightn't be totally serious. But as we sat on his veranda in the pale sun of a winter's morning, drinking the buyer's sample cup of his Arabica coffee, he did have a killer's glint in his eye. 'If I could get away with it scot-free, I'd do it, no problem,' he said quietly.

Over and around us settled the usual sharp, hot aroma of burnt toast, which gradually intensified into the smell of overheated brake linings. I used to think it came from the long-distance trucks hurtling through the murderously sharp curves and steep hills of the Pacific Highway a couple of kilometres away. Eric's farm sometimes smells like the highway at Easter, especially when holidaymakers' cars are competing with interstate truck-transport schedules. But nowadays I know it's just his beans roasting in the processing shed.

Despite the burnt-rubber smell, I'd dropped in to buy a bag of his organic coffee beans. I like the idea of consuming local produce and supporting neighbourhood farmers. We've been friends since I designed the website for his business, The Coastal Coffee Company, with links to Callahan Plantations and Callahan's Rainforest Fruits. Because I work from home my hours are flexible and I need an occasional break from the computer and the solitude. Anyway, I wanted to see how he was bearing up.

The volcanic soil starts at the ridge line near Eric's plantations. In this rich red dirt he's always experimenting with some interesting fruit or crop. As well as marketing his produce, he has a little stall out the front to attract the passing drivers to his pecan and macadamia nuts, nuggety avocados, breadfruit, mangoes, custard apples, mysterious knobbly-looking citrus, and Cavendish and ladyfinger bananas at

THE LIFE ALIGNMENT OF THE COFFEE GROWER

pre-Cyclone Anna prices. His stall works on the honour system. You drop coins into a slot in a metal pipe he's cemented to the ground, and on Friday evenings he collects the coins (arriving at the pub with heavy jangling pockets) and he's got his weekend beer money.

As a matter of geographical interest, our region falls into a unique and bewildering zone varying between Pacific maritime and dry hinterland (running east–west), and between tropical and temperate (running north–south). This also depends, of course, on the prevailing winds being southerly or northerly, or variations on these. Because this is the most easterly point of the continent, sometimes we have several climates at once. We experience electrical storms that, without warning, send telephone conversationalists flying backwards across their lounge rooms. This year we had a tornado that selectively razed the church and the school, and an abrupt spring storm with hailstones like oranges that concussed several competitors in the local bowling club's championship mixed pairs. All this means that imaginative farmers like Eric are never quite sure whether a particular new crop will succeed.

Eric's more exotic experiments have been less successful than they would have been 500 kilometres north. (His mangosteens, Chinese raisins and ice-cream beans were a disaster.) Nonetheless, he boasts about his coffee being the southernmost coffee in the world, and claims that this extremity of latitude and ground temperature gives it less caffeine than Brazilian, Kenyan, Colombian or New Guinean beans. He says in these health-conscious times this is a good marketing ploy. I admire his optimism. You certainly don't feel jumpy after drinking Eric's coffee. But if murder's on your mind, I guess that's a good thing.

A cane fire was burning down on the patchwork quilt of sugarcane flats, and as we drank our coffee we watched the smoke spiralling straight up into the sky like a water spout. In the blue haze there was no smoke drift in any direction, no clouds, no hawks or swifts high in the sky, no breeze to rustle the leaves in Eric's plantations, no diversion to determine a change of topic. Within three or four minutes the flames had died and the smoke had vanished but the bitter subject of murder still hung in the air.

Eric said, 'I wouldn't want any palaver like in the movies.

No big discussion about the whys and wherefores. I'd just like the bastard to know he was going to cark it.'

I'll admit that when Eric makes a cup of coffee from his own roasted beans it tastes better than when I do. One day I'll master the subtleties of his beans and make an acceptable pot. Eventually I said, 'You're kidding, of course.'

'You reckon?' He sighed and shook the dregs of his cup into the bougainvillea. Then he stretched, flexed his arms and rolled his shoulders around like a weary old heavyweight boxer.

You get a reasonable impression of a person when you're designing their website. In the preparation beforehand their vanities and the attributes they want to stress on the World Wide Web tend to throw into sharp relief those things they want glossed over. Personality defects. Professional lapses. Missing years in the curriculum vitae. The fact that their coffee lacks oomph and they want to kill someone.

Considering Eric in the context of first-degree murder, the coffee grower as would-be killer, he was thickset, long-armed, monobrowed and physically threatening. You could believe him capable of killing someone, with his bare hands if necessary. But viewed merely as an organic farmer with a broken heart, he came across that solemn windless morning, as a heavy sad-eyed fellow who believed marriage worked on the honour system, too.

'At the very least I'd like Dolphin Boy to suffer something disfiguring,' he said. 'Apart from the ordinary busted nose and knocked-out teeth. Something that'd put her off him.'

By *her*, he was referring to Jeannie, his wife of nineteen years, who'd recently begun what she announced was 'a spiritual journey' with a man with only one name, like Madonna and Pink and Bono. The boyfriend's chosen name was Sargasso, like the fabled seaweedy sea, graveyard of ships and birthplace of eels. He was a painter of frangipanis and hibiscuses and lurid sunsets and rainbows arching into the ocean. But Sargasso's big money-spinner was dolphins: dolphins at dawn, dolphins at dusk, dolphins surfing the point break, and dolphins spiralling up towards vivid cartoon rainbows that curled over a benign sea. All up and down the east coast you'd see his distinctive dolphin paintings displayed in beach boutiques and cafes, on the walls of motel rooms and dentists and real estate agents. Dolphins sold. I reckon a dolphin could get elected to parliament in some of those towns.

When she departed, Jeannie had announced, 'I'm heartily sick of the smell of coffee.' Apart from coffee in all its varieties and blends, her new quest also disdained alcohol, meat, dairy products, newspapers and any books without an Eastern spiritual basis. I'd seen Sargasso around the district for years: a loose-limbed, lean, perpetually tanned type who displayed a bare torso long past summer and encouraged his abundant wavy hair in the style of Charles II. The fluid, flirting, drawstring-trousers-and-no-underwear sort, first on the floor when the music starts, last to get off, hips like a lizard, who arouses general male animosity the moment he steps out his front door. Women love him.

Suddenly Eric pointed towards the coastline, beyond those coffee and macadamia rows he'd planted and trimmed as neatly as a Bali tourist's hair braids. 'The love shack,' he said, grimly. On the crest of the hill stood a lone stone house with a Bangalow palm on either side: Sargasso's cottage. Its white-painted tin roof stood out from the lantana-covered escarpment and hazy sky. As the present object of attention it seemed to be preening in its own personal sunrays. Purple and white Tibetan prayer flags hung motionless outside, and Jeannie's distinctive yellow Volvo station wagon was nudged in between them, nuzzling the flagpoles. My own imagination was working overtime, so Eric's mind must have been going haywire. He wiped a hand across his eyes and swore vigorously. 'I could do the bastard with one hand behind my back,' he said.

It was two nights later, after the usual Friday evening pub session, that Eric drove over the hill, shouldered past the prayer flags, burst through the door of the love shack and caught his wife and Sargasso together. He stood there in the doorway, the day's red dirt still on his work boots, and stared at them. They stared back. They were painting pictures of frangipanis and drinking tea.

On the table in front of the painters were three saucers, one each of floating white, yellow and pink frangipani blossoms, like a religious offering, and the flowers' sweet bruised smell filled the cottage. As Eric told me later, 'It's impossible to raise a finger against someone drinking tea.' He'd suddenly felt foolish standing on an unfamiliar threshold that smelled of flowers, in front of his estranged wife. But not as stupid as if he'd swung a punch at a still-life frangipani painter.

~~~

Niche farmers need to have their wits about them. Depending on the state of the market and trends in food, and making allowances for extreme weather, pests and disease, to survive they have to move fast from one crop, one fruit, one stock animal, to another. When we next had the opportunity for a personal conversation (I don't like to pry, and anyway the public bar on Friday night is the last place for meaningful talk), Eric was sitting on his veranda chewing a chicken leg and fretting about his nut.

'The nut's a big worry,' he said. I should mention that around these parts, nuts are *nut* singular. As in, 'Do you grow nut?' Most nut is macadamia, but it doesn't matter which kind — macadamias, pecans, walnuts, Brazil, almonds — or if you've got 10 000 fully laden trees; they're all *nut*. Like with wild animals in Africa, you use the singular or appear hopelessly naive. When in Kenya it's advisable to say, 'Look at those *zebra* and *giraffe*!' even if there are 200 of them galloping past. Being chased by five *lion*. The same up here with nut.

Eric said, 'Wouldn't you know it?' Just as the banana market had dropped again and he'd ploughed his ladyfingers under, and turned that particular hillside over to another 500 macadamias, there was a sudden twelve per cent fall in nut. He wasn't the only farmer affected. Before global macadamia prices began looking shaky, this whole region swung over to nut. Eric sounded mournfully wise now. 'You want the history of nut? It used to be just the city farmers needing a tax break. And lawyers and doctors wanting a hobby farm without much labour attached. Then suddenly the nut became highly profitable. America, Asia – everyone wanted our nut. The big boys, the corporations, moved in. Now just about every old cow paddock and orchard is totally nut.'

Fortunately Eric wasn't completely nut. He still had his organic coffee – chemical-free, not genetically modified, gentle on the stomach and blood pressure. He had his mangoes, too, and dwarf avocados and knotty-looking tangelos – and he'd stuck with Cavendish bananas, the long ones. But the decline of the nut coincided with some heavy personal blows.

THE LIFE ALIGNMENT OF THE COFFEE GROWER

Last summer he'd burnt his hand in a coffee-roasting accident. Next thing his old mother died of Alzheimer's down in Sydney and, being of unsound mind, left him out of her will. To top it off, Jeannie announced she was embarking on her 'personal journey'. Not much travel involved on that trip, just a 300-metre drive over the hill to a white-roofed stone cottage.

In Eric's mind, all his troubles came together in the permanently nut-brown figure of Sargasso the dolphin painter; the wavy-haired poseur who'd named himself after a seaweedy sea that was the graveyard of ships and the birthplace of eels. It was nothing to do with me, but I found myself disliking him, too.

Eric's a basic type of man. For months he stamped around the place raging at anything that reminded him, even vaguely, of the enemy. Everything from marine mammals to yoga was the subject of his wrath. Of course violent reprisals were still contemplated against Sargasso, at the very least the rearrangement of his House-of-Stuart-meets-the-rainforest features. But as the days passed, reason prevailed, and instead Eric lapsed into melancholy and Margaret River cabernet. A lonely year limped along, the time passing in anxious nut reflection and review. Once twelve months had gone, however, as if by some telepathic signal, those female friends who hadn't sided with Jeannie's journey began matchmaking on his behalf.

Eric was intrigued at first, even a little excited. Until he met the match-ups. Without exception, his female friends chose for him capable, financially independent country women with ethical histories, no addictions and minimal emotional baggage. 'Decent ladies, all of them,' he explained. 'Heads on straight, imaginative kitchen skills, adept at keeping the books or whipping up a bouillabaisse. But the sort I might choose if I was looking for an aunt rather than a girlfriend.'

However, here we were drinking beer and nibbling drumsticks on Eric's veranda, at the first party since the marriage split, on hand to meet a woman he'd chosen himself for a romantic relationship. 'This is Desiree,' he announced, somewhat shyly, waving an organic chicken leg as she drifted towards us. It must be said that Desiree was attractive in an ageless way. She was wearing a pink caftan that tipped the floor, and bare feet with a couple of rings on her toes, and her hand felt boneless and cool as she insisted on reading the lines in our palms. Then she inquired after everyone's star sign.

THE LIFE ALIGNMENT OF THE COFFEE GROWER

I was staggered. Although she was seductively willowy and smelled like freesias, she seemed to represent everything he'd come to detest. And Eric did look faintly embarrassed. Overriding the astrology chatter, he declared, loudly and distractedly, 'I'm confident the nut will come back.' He gestured down towards his macadamias lined up in their dark military ranks. 'It'll be back by Christmas.'

Desiree wagged an admonishing finger. She padded up to him and squeezed his shoulder. 'Nuts. Nuts. Nuts. He's such a Taurean!'

※

After a few months Desiree moved in with Eric and, as far as I could tell, life at The Coastal Coffee Company (and Callahan Plantations and Callahan's Rainforest Fruits) was settled and rosy. Whenever I crossed paths with Eric he wore a faintly bemused smile and I could only imagine that Desiree was good for him. Then our region was beset by weeks of unusually wild weather, marked by fierce winds and extremes of temperature. Frosts covered the valleys night and day.

Five-metre waves pounded the coast and the rivers turned red with mud. Eric was one person, though, who didn't need to rely on the latest Severe Storm Warning from the Bureau of Meteorology. He knew the weather was going to turn nasty when Doug Anthony descended from the rafters and slumped on top of the television set.

Doug was a two-metre carpet python, named after the former Deputy Prime Minister of Australia, who used to be Eric's local member of parliament or, as he referred to him, 'my lord of the manor'. Doug Anthony had long since left the political arena but Eric always called his resident pythons after him as a mark of respect.

In the vibrations of the power lines, Doug Anthony could anticipate by several hours the first hints of the cyclonic wind that would soon be whistling through the eaves. Long before the first tremors began in the roof, Doug Anthony, unnerved and cross, sought the ground-floor warmth and security of the television – at least until the storm broke and the power blacked out, or he slid off the TV set. (He was a big boy; there was a fair amount of tail and belly overlap.) Then he slithered off disconsolately towards refuge in the linen cupboard.

'Doug looks exhausted,' Eric told me, over the usual sample cup of coffee on his veranda. 'He needs his winter sleep but he's not getting enough.' Nor was Eric, it turned out. Until Doug returned to the rafters – out of sight, out of mind – Desiree had moved out of home.

After some animated discussion, in which Eric pointed out that a resident python was necessary on a macadamia farm to keep down the rats, and that he lost eight per cent of his crop to rats even *with* Doug, he'd been forced to cart Doug off to the nearest patch of rainforest. But pythons won't do things they don't want to. Having spent the whole twelve years of his existence dining effortlessly on the plentiful vermin at The Coastal Coffee Company, Doug was back the next day, lying pathetically along the doorstep like a lumpy draught-stopper, with a fruit-bat-shaped bulge in his middle. He had no intention of leaving home, which left Desiree no choice.

During this extreme weather, Eric was in a nervous state just keeping his equipment, crops and orchards intact, without the Desiree-versus-Doug stand-off. All the local farmers were shocked by the minus-nine-degrees nights that froze the stone-fruit on the trees, turned the unripe strawberries and blueberries as soft and pulpy as jam, and left the mangoes and avocados as hard as cricket balls. The winds stripped the unripe nuts from their branches and fired them like bruising grapeshot against the fruit trees. Orchardists tried pumping water from the creek to spray their fruit trees overnight to keep them warm, but the record frost defeated them and next morning stalactites hung off the branches.

Eric explained that Doug was supposed to be hibernating, not roaming about the house seeking warm and motionless resting spots. 'He wound himself around the top of the chimney for a month, clinging on for dear life. Then we had that strange sunny spell and he spent every day sunbaking on the ping-pong table on the veranda. The unbroken warm days confused him and made him think it was summer. He was shedding skin and looking frisky and suddenly next-door's cat disappeared. Then we had those cyclonic winds, and trees blew down, and the house shook, and Doug was too nervy to sleep up in the rafters.'

A resident python wasn't the only wildlife specimen feeling out of sorts. When the weather turned windy and wet, the cane toads came out of hibernation too soon, the

THE LIFE ALIGNMENT OF THE COFFEE GROWER

house spiders arrived unheralded in the bathrooms, and the huntsmen began hunting all across the ceilings. In the middle of winter, the water dragons appeared, bemused, out of the shrubbery, glanced quickly around and vanished again. Meanwhile, the male brush turkeys had long since built their nesting mounds only to have them and the unhatched eggs swept away in the latest deluge. Always flustered, the brush turkeys were frenetic with worry.

The natural environment was behaving unseasonably and erratically. Bull sharks started entering our muddy rivers and travelling upstream, bumping against boats and scaring fishermen and kayakers. Early-season fleas climbed our trouser legs, and the region's primary-school scalps began teeming with nits at least one term too early. Houses reeked of flea bombs and LiceBlaster. In the meantime, as Eric showed me, Doug Anthony was curled up on top of the TV guide, his skin patterns blurry and sallow, the tip of his tail flopping over half the screen, looking sorry for himself.

'Doug is very sensitive. He can taste the changes in the weather with his tongue,' Eric said. 'And he's not happy.' Neither was Eric. This was clear from his fidgety demeanour.

He was fond of Doug, what with his antecedents and pest-disposal habits, but he was missing Desiree. The climate of Eric's existence was definitely changeable.

≈

'How's life?' I ventured, sipping one of Eric's quadruple-strength Arabica espressos, whose kick almost equals a single shot anywhere else. We were sitting on the steps of his roasting shed, the aroma of burnt beans soaking into our clothes and skin. Whenever I drive away from The Coastal Coffee Company I think I've left the handbrake on.

'Much better,' he answered. 'Doug's back up in the rafters again so Desiree came home last week. I guess I can't complain.'

But he still looked a bit edgy. After a moment, he said, 'Desiree has laid down some new ground rules for staying with me.'

'Ground rules?'

'Rules on the way things have to be arranged in future. What's it called? Chop suey? Mah jong? You know what I mean. She's making me do things with my shoes in Chinese.'

THE LIFE ALIGNMENT OF THE COFFEE GROWER

There was another long moment while I sipped my coffee. Eventually I had a brainwave. 'You don't mean *feng shui*?'

'That's it. She's always checking that my shoes aren't facing the wall. She says shoes have to be turned facing into the room, otherwise their owner will never be free.' He gave an embarrassed laugh. 'Even if they're sitting in the cupboard. And I've got to chuck out all my old boots from the garage. She hates the garage. She says it represents emotions from the past. And here's me thinking it represented a roof over the ute.'

Those of us who know Eric were anticipating something like this. Eric is a conservative farmer. Desiree teaches Life Alignment. Eric grows difficult produce often best suited to other regions. Desiree balances negative energies for a living. If you're suffering from an enemy's curses or geopathic stress, she's your woman.

'She says I should always see my feet as indicators of where they can take me,' Eric said.

'Makes sense,' I said.

'Best foot forward and all that,' said Eric.

'Absolutely.'

Eric was staring off across the macadamia fields towards

the white-roofed cottage of the painter of frangipanis and dolphins. He blinked then, as if to switch his flow of thought, and went on, his voice low. 'Desiree has a thing about keys, too. If you want a new life you have to throw away the keys you no longer use or the ones associated with anyone else. They have to be kept in descending order of size. One short key and one long key next to each other on your key ring means your life will be like a roller-coaster. Keys facing different ways will keep you always heading in different ways, too.'

'Not if you're careful with your shoe direction.'

'Don't try joking with Desiree about this stuff.'

'Things are OK between you, aren't they?'

'Well, they are compared to when a carpet python was curled up in the lounge room. *And* pointing the wrong way.' And now he laughed. 'A two-metre snake living on the TV set really wrecks the *feng shui*.'

We finished our coffee, I picked up my bag of beans and a selection of his exotic fruits, their spottiness, skin lumps and irregular size pointing out their organic origins, and I started to leave.

'I don't believe in that stuff for a second,' he said quietly.

'But when I'm undressing I turn my boots around, even if she's not watching. I've tossed out all my old keys. Look, it can't hurt.'

〰️

For a few months, thanks to Desiree's stern *feng shui* principles relating to shoes, keys and indoor pythons, Eric's life seemed on the upturn. Then came the pronouncement the countryside was both dreading and wishing for: details of the long-proposed Pacific Highway upgrade.

After a decade, the new route was finally announced – a major realignment to wipe out the notorious curves and hills between Woodburn and Ballina, and Tintenbar and Byron Bay. It would allow even more trucks, carrying heavier loads, to hurtle faster between Sydney and Brisbane. Apart from abetting the destruction – so its opponents alleged – of fifty threatened fauna species, including the Coxen's fig parrot and Albert's lyrebird, and one of the region's few remaining healthy koala populations, the upgraded highway would wipe out 1000 hectares of farmland.

Eric learnt that his land would be cut in half and he'd lose a twenty-hectare strip of coffee bushes, fruit and macadamia trees right down the middle. The authorities assured him, however, that his farmhouse would not be bulldozed. Instead it would be separated from his plantations by six lanes of speeding traffic. In order to tend his land each day, and roast his coffee beans, he'd have to drive ten kilometres, then cross the highway via an overpass or roundabout. As recompense for the noise and inconvenience, the Roads and Traffic Authority had offered to provide double-glazing for his windows.

This was one piece of life alignment beyond even Desiree's talents. For three days Eric retreated to the pub to consider fate's various configurations over neatly lined-up schooners of Coopers Draught. The sudden peril facing the Coxen's fig parrot and Albert's lyrebird did not move him unduly (the parrot's name was a bit of a giveaway); as an orchardist he saw all birds, if not as the enemy, then definitely as collaborators. But he had a soft spot for koalas and was sorry they'd be sharing the latest episode in his saga of rotten luck.

The highway-through-his-land decision joined the list of

THE LIFE ALIGNMENT OF THE COFFEE GROWER

misfortunes he'd had to bear over the past year, beginning with Jeannie's journey to the cottage of that snake-hipped painter of dolphins and frangipanis. His mother dying; the brouhaha over her will; his burnt hand in the coffee roaster; the drop in macadamia prices – as he saw it, this litany of bad luck could be sheeted home to bloody Sargasso, the name-thief of the graveyard of ships and the birthplace of eels, who'd also stolen his wife.

By now Eric had had a big enough serving of what life was currently dishing out. A protest was planned against the highway upgrade and he decided to join it. So it was arranged. A convoy of angry farmers driving tractors, farm trucks, bulldozers and a prime mover assembled outside Byron Bay, to crawl at fifteen kilometres an hour along the Pacific Highway to Ballina, where a petition of thousands of protesting signatures would be submitted to the government.

Eric drove his tractor. He was feeling so righteous that for once he experienced a bonding with the parrot- and marsupial-loving environmentalists also gathered at the assembly point. Weren't they all in this together? As the convoy moved off, people in koala suits enthusiastically indicated with their furry paws and muffled voices that they'd like to join in the farmers' protest. 'Jump aboard!' yelled Eric to one eager koala and, with the traffic already banking up behind them, they set off down the highway.

At fifteen kilometres an hour, under a rigid police escort, two sets of buttocks pressed together on the one metal tractor seat, it was a very long two and a half hours to Ballina. Especially when Eric's passenger, sweating from the heat after only ten minutes, took off his koala head.

'We need to talk, man,' said Sargasso.

Acknowledgements

EARLY FRAGMENTS OF some of these stories first appeared in *A2*, *The Age* magazine, for which I thank the editors, especially Sally Heath and Liza Power.

'The Lap Pool', 'The Aquarium at Night' and 'How to Kill a Cane Toad' were first published in *Meanjin*; 'The Water Person and the Tree Person' in *Griffith Review* and *The Weekend Australian Magazine*; 'Stones Like Hearts' in *Lines in the Sand*, the seventieth-anniversary anthology of the Fellowship of Australian Writers, Western Australia; and 'The Life Alignment of the Coffee Grower' in *Rusty's Byron Guide*.

For important reasons, my thanks to Fiona Daniels and my daughter Amy.

'The Whale Watchers' is by way of homage to John Cheever's story 'Reunion'.

ALSO BY ROBERT DREWE

Grace

Some relevant facts about Grace Molloy. Apart from being named after a 100 000-year-old skeleton, she was twenty-nine and for much of the past three years she'd been hiding from an erotomaniac.

Physically and emotionally besieged, Grace attempts to claw back her personal territory by abandoning her inner-city life as a film reviewer and fleeing to the remoteness of the Kimberley – where existence and territory have altogether wider implications. Lying low, working in a wildlife park, she slowly reclaims her sanity. Her only links to the outside world are her father and her stalker.

Intricately plotted, breathlessly paced, *Grace* reflects on the countless varieties of love and the nature of fear. At once intimate and grand in scale, this disquieting and provocatively witty novel reveals the full vigour of an artistic vision in turn poetic and cinematic.

'Drewe is one of the most significant novelists currently working.'
The Guardian

'Superbly written and utterly absorbing, *Grace* resonates
long after the last page has been turned.'
Vogue

'An embarrassment of riches from one of our greatest storytellers.'
Sunday Telegraph

'*Grace* is like a flare of hope in an empty sea.'
The West Australian

The Shark Net

Aged six, Robert Drewe moved with his family from Melbourne to Perth, the world's most isolated city – and proud of it. This sun-baked coast was innocently proud, too, of its tranquillity and friendliness.

Then a man he knew murdered a boy he also knew. The murderer randomly killed eight strangers – variously shooting, strangling, stabbing, bludgeoning and hacking his victims and running them down with cars – and innocent Perth was changed forever.

In the middle-class suburbs which were the killer's main stalking grounds, the mysterious murders created widespread anxiety and instant local myth. *'The murders and their aftermath have both intrigued me and weighed heavily on me for three decades. To try to make sense of this time and place, and of my own childhood and adolescence, I had, finally, to write about it.'*

The result is *The Shark Net*, a vibrant and haunting memoir that reaches beyond the dark recesses of murder and chaos to encompass their ordinary suburban backdrop. *The Shark Net* shows one of Australia's most acclaimed writers charting new and exciting territory.

'Fascinating . . . A moving and unpretentious memoir of
a precocious youth, a bittersweet tribute to youth's optimism.'
Joyce Carol Oates, *New York Review of Books*

'An instant classic . . . Constructed with superb craftsmanship,
written with precision and tough humour, and with an extraordinary
story to tell, it seems certain to enjoy a long life.'
Randolph Stow, *Times Literary Supplement*

The Drowner

In the warm alkaline waters of the public bath a headstrong young engineer accidentally collides with a beautiful actress. From this innocent collision of flesh begins a passion that takes them from the Wiltshire Downs to the most elemental choices of life and death in the Australian desert. Their intense romance is but part of the daring story that unfolds. Mingling history, myth and technology with a modern cinematic and poetic imagination, Robert Drewe presents a fable of European ambitions in an alien landscape, and a magnificently sustained metaphor of water as the life-and-death force.

Winner of seven national prizes for literature, including the New South Wales Premier's Book of the Year award and the Adelaide Festival Prize for Literature.

'Myth, magic and melody coalesce in a fertile delta of the imagination. Spellbinding.'
Sunday Times

'Drewe's writing is cinematically immediate and crackles with an intensity of sense . . . A mesmeric and utterly addictive book.'
Independent on Sunday

'Drewe is a profoundly elegant writer. His magnificent novel is the best thing I have read this year.'
Sunday Tribune, Dublin

'Full of incident, oddity, humanity and poetry . . . This is in the true sense a delightful book.'
Thomas Keneally

The Bodysurfers

Set among the surf and sandhills of the Australian beach – and the tidal changes of three generations of the Lang family – this bestselling collection of short stories is an Australian classic. *The Bodysurfers* vividly evokes the beach, with the scent of suntan oil, the sting of the sun and a lazy sensuality, all the while hinting at a deep undercurrent of suburban malaise.

From its first publication, these poignant and seductive stories marked a major change in Australian literature.

'These stories breathe. Taut yet teeming with life, seductive yet stylistically chaste, they are shot through with gritty phrases that catch at one's throat.'
The Sydney Morning Herald

'A remarkably seductive and exuberant collection which manages, in its portrayal of human relationships, to be both mordant in tone and playful in manner.'
Times Literary Supplement

'*The Bodysurfers* is a brilliant book. It is clever, touching and at times desperately funny.'
Canberra Times

'His characters repeatedly hurl themselves at life and lovers. There is something very poignant about these stories.'
Newsweek

Our Sunshine

Our Sunshine is the tale of a man whose story outgrew his life. Robert Drewe's strikingly imaginative re-creation of the inner life of Ned Kelly, the National Hero and Devil Incarnate of the Antipodes, is written with brilliant clarity and impressionistic economy. It carries the reader into a dreamworld of astonishing and violent revelation, an entrancing and frightening landscape of murder, sexuality, persecution, robbery, vanity, politics and corruption.

'This is a mesmerising novel.'
Times Literary Supplement

'This book is addictive. Drewe's language is, as ever, astonishing, with every one of his sentences containing a shiver of exactness and immediacy.'
New Statesman

'A *tour de force* . . . A model of style and passion.'
The Age

'Drewe has performed a remarkable feat of literary sleight-of-hand . . . *Our Sunshine* is a marvellous book.'
Sydney Morning Herald

read more
my penguin e-newsletter

Subscribe to receive *read more*, your monthly e-newsletter from Penguin Australia. As a *read more* subscriber you'll receive sneak peeks of new books, be kept up to date with what's hot, have the opportunity to meet your favourite authors, download reading guides for your book club, receive special offers, be in the running to win exclusive subscriber-only prizes, plus much more.

Visit penguin.com.au/readmore to subscribe